In this highly anticipated conclusion to *Blood and Damnation*, cursed vampire Marcus St. James must choose between wrath and retribution—or love.

Following a lead from a seer, Marcus St. James left Victorian England and has landed in Havenwood Falls, still searching for Catriona, the girl who'd managed to break through his fortress and ensnare his heart. He's been searching for her for over a year, since the night she was captured by gypsies and stolen away. But it seems he and his trusted assistant Knox have traveled halfway around the world only to arrive at a dead end.

Cursed to exist as a blood-drinker, Marcus is no stranger to gossip and speculation, so when dead bodies start appearing in Havenwood Falls, he is immediately under suspicion. With two telltale vampire fang marks scarring each body, fear begins to circulate, bringing his own investigation into Catriona's whereabouts to a grinding halt.

But once the dust starts to settle, a new discovery threatens to shatter his world, forcing Marcus to make his most devastating choice yet. Will he forgo his thirst for retribution and abandon justice to keep the peace? Or will his wrath be his undoing and leave him forever cursed?

LEGENDS OF HAVENWOOD FALLS BOOKS

Lost in Time by Tish Thawer

Dawn of the Witch Hunters by Morgan Wylie

Redemption's End by Eric R. Asher

Trapped Within a Wish by Brynn Myers

Blood and Damnation by Belinda Boring

Fated Beginnings by E.J. Fechenda

Emeline by Katie M. John

Released From a Curse by Brynn Myers

A Pack of Lies by Kallie Ross

Kiss the Ashes by Desiree Lafawn

Hidden Truths by Colleen Nye

Wrath and Retribution by Belinda Boring

Changing Fate by Char Webster

Rise of the Witch Hunters by Morgan Wylie

The Drowning Bride by Seven Jane

Also try the main Havenwood Falls series; the YA line, Havenwood Falls High; the darker, sexier side of town, Havenwood Falls Sin & Silk; and the local supernatural college, Sun & Moon Academy.

Stay up to date at www.HavenwoodFalls.com

ALSO BY BELINDA BORING

THE MYSTIC WOLVES SERIES

The Mystic Wolves

Forget Me Not

Testing Fate

Forever Changed

Savage Possession

Darkness Unleashed

Last Wolf Standing

Blood Oath

A Very Mystic Christmas (Collection of Christmas Memories)

DAMAGED SOULS SERIES

Bittersweet Melody

Bittersweet Symphony

Enchanted Heart

Loving Liberty

Broken Promises

From My Heart To Yours

HAVENWOOD FALLS TITLES

Nowhere to Hide

Addicted to You (Sequel to Nowhere to Hide)

Blood & Damnation (Legends of Havenwood Falls)

The Collector: Awakening

Short Story Anthology 2018

Wrath & Retribution (Sequel to Blood & Damnation)

WRATH AND RETRIBUTION
A LEGENDS OF HAVENWOOD FALLS NOVELLA

BELINDA BORING

To my sister from another mister, Laura Benedict.

Thank you for being such a wonderfully supportive friend and someone to go on adventures with! Don't ever change! Love you!

PROLOGUE

CATRIONA

1879

The brisk night air felt like a rough slap across my face.

After weeks of endless travel, we'd finally come to what I hoped was the end of our grueling journey. Not that our sudden stop would aid my escape. I was in no condition to flee—to gather up my tattered rags of a skirt and run as though the Devil himself was after me.

Days had stopped making sense in my jumbled thoughts. The months had long since blended into one another, and although I'd valiantly tried to keep track in the beginning, the world was merely a haze of places and strange faces.

There was a small part of me that tried to remain brave and strong. It was from there that a voice whispered to not give up hope, because my husband would find me. Marcus St. James. How the mere thought of him had roused my spirits in the beginning.

Now, a more sinister feeling crept around the edges of my mind —delivering the sober truth that no one was going to rescue me, because I wasn't something he treasured. Should Marcus and Knox indeed find me all the way across the sea, it would be for the sole purpose of satisfying his thirst for vengeance.

No matter how hard I struggled to keep that realization from taking root, the evidence became clearer and clearer as time continued to blur by. He'd once told me I was his property. It was foolish to cling to my heart's hope that he'd grown to care for me.

A brusque female voice broke through my despondent musings. "Is this her?"

I was roughly pulled off the horse, my captor's strong grip wrapped around my arm.

He grunted in response, shoving me hard so I stood within the light's faint halo. "Can you take her?"

My heart skipped a beat. Was this finally the end of the road—an end to the harrowing journey the gypsy had taken me on?

England felt so far away as I slowly looked up and found myself under the intense scrutiny of a dark-haired woman. My gaze quickly darted up and took in my surroundings. Dusk was now upon us, and the night air was filled with the sounds of people heading home for the day. Not this building, however. More light spilled out from the plain glassed windows, seeping out through the lace curtains that hung within.

Piano music unlike any I'd heard before echoed about, matched only by the cheery sounds of chatter and laughter. If I was to wager a guess, my captor had brought me to a saloon or some kind of establishment that catered to drinking and pleasures. We'd stopped at enough along the way for me to recognize the telltale scent of ale and whiskey.

I was definitely a long way from home and the sheltered life I'd been brought up in.

The woman began her slow catlike stalking around me, and suddenly, I felt very, very naked beneath her gaze.

"I have no use for more girls," she tutted as her lips pursed in thought. "Unless you believe she has a talent to please." Without warning, the strange lady grabbed hold of my face, her fingers squeezing my chin until I squirmed in pain. "Do you still have your virtue?"

Part of me wanted to scream . . . wanted to reach out and slap her hard. Once upon a time I would've scratched out her eyes, fought tooth and nail to be free from both of them, but that was then, and this was now. Wisdom was needed—courage—to survive.

I shook my head and looked at my captor, Dimitri. My own personal monster had a name, one he'd boasted in sharing the second he knew we were free from England and his revenge had been successful.

For the briefest of moments, I thought I caught a glimpse of compassion in her eyes. Dimitri was a hulk of a man with a dark piercing stare that caused other men to give him a wide berth. The woman had assumed rightly that he'd taken from my body what he wanted, and that he was far from a gentle lover.

Those were memories I buried deep inside me—far away from the light of day where they wouldn't drive me insane. There were many things I locked away now. The only memory I entertained was Marcus's shout into the night air that he would find me.

I knew that made me a fool, but my stubbornness was the only thing I had left. My pride had been stripped away with each of Dimitri's rough touches.

"She is for my pleasure alone," he responded, slapping me hard on the behind. Gritting my teeth, I forced myself not to cringe or fall to the ground from the force. I still didn't know whether this new woman would become my new jailor or indeed my salvation. I wouldn't show her weakness. I wouldn't show her how completely broken I felt.

"If I take her on, and that is a huge if, Dimitri, I ask that you not manhandle the poor thing." The gypsy male easily towered over her, yet she showed no fear as she pointed her finger, chastising him. Wrapping her arm around my shoulder, she did the unthinkable. For the first time since this whole ordeal begun, someone protected me. "I'll do this because of our family."

And then, as the conversation broke down into a familiar language, my stomach dropped, and my fragile hope was shattered yet again.

Romani.

She wouldn't become my savior or someone I could possibly win over and earn my freedom from. The more I stared at the woman, the easier it was to see the similarities she shared with Dimitri. There was no mistaking that they were kin. The false sense of security that had begun to blossom within me shriveled and died like a neglected rose beneath a cruel sun.

I stared down at the ground and wrapped my arms tightly around myself, hoping to keep the chill from shaking me into pieces. The harder I tried, though, the stronger the quaking became. I was just so tired—exhausted from trying to remain brave. Tears began to flow down my cheeks. They were a luxury I refused to allow myself, but as the sound of their heated conversation broke against me, I lowered my guard and the pain swept in.

Tears for me.

Tears for my future.

Tears for the life that I'd been cruelly ripped from. Never would I complain again about Marcus and his neglect. My heart longed to be back at Smithersby Field—to be standing outside the door to his office where I'd faithfully knocked, hoping to be admitted. I would welcome back that uncertainty a hundred times over if it meant that I could be safe within his home.

"Look, you have made her cry, you oaf," the woman blurted, finally turning her attention back to me. The look of compassion had returned to her face—features I'd only just judged as kind, but now couldn't believe. Even as she gently wiped away my tears with the lace handkerchief she pulled out from the front of her bosom, I steeled my resolve. If she was related to Dimitri, then she couldn't be trusted. She was simply another threat to endure.

Pushing past her, Dimitri grabbed me once more and shook me by the arm.

"You're to stay here until I return." His demand was delivered with enough force not to brook any argument. I already knew that any disobedience would incur his anger.

I nodded quickly and returned my gaze to the floor. Submission pleased him. It always hurt less when I pleased him.

He barked out something else in Romani before swinging his leg up and over his horse. Dimitri was going to leave me here— leave me alone for the first time in a year. Traveling from England, he masqueraded us as a married couple, playing the overly protective husband. There hadn't been more than a few seconds where I wasn't being watched by him, yet now he rode off into the night without a single glance back.

The thought of being here in this strange place alone would've once excited me with all the possibilities for adventures. Now, it sent another round of tremors through my body, weakening my knees to the point I staggered forward and clutched onto my new jailor.

"You are safe for now," the woman whispered as she steadied me back on my feet. She remained quiet until I eventually looked up and found her waiting. Now that Dimitri was gone, I studied her.

Her dark hair was pinned back from her face into a loose bun that had pretty white flowers threaded through the strands. I imagined her the age of my mother, had she survived the pox that had rampaged through our small town when I was still a young child. Her cheeks were reddened, and I couldn't tell if it was from the chilly air kissing her skin or because she was a woman who wore rouge. Unlike mine, her clothing was beautifully stitched, fitting her form perfectly.

"My name is Mrs. Fanny Webster, and this is my home." She gestured back to the building where music still flowed from. That wasn't what confused me, however. She must've been used to people responded to her name because she broke out into laughter. "That is my English name. I adopted a more appropriate one when I arrived in this great country. In my family, what you are called holds certain power, and in the case of the Romani, it often generates fear and hatred."

All I could do was nod in agreement. I'd seen that same emotion consume Marcus—his loathing for gypsies was deep-seated and overshadowed his life. His wrath was at least justified, because of the curse he bore as a result of dealing with them. I'd also seen that same skepticism in the strangers I encountered with Dimitri.

"So," I spoke, my voice soft and scratchy from the lack of use, "you are to be my new owner?"

This earned me another round of laughter, this time louder and heartier than before. "Do you desire that?" She reached to brush aside a strand of hair, and this time I did flinch. I wasn't used to being shown such kindness. "What shall I call you?"

"Catriona," I answered reluctantly.

"Well, Catriona, while you are not free to leave, you are not prisoner here in my home. You will simply stay with me until Dimitri returns." She said it so matter-of-factly, as though the lies that came rolling off her tongue didn't bother her.

"I believe that's the very definition of being owned, Mrs. Webster," I uttered, surprised at my brazenness. I waited, breath held, for the slap that would've followed such a retort to Dimitri, but none came.

"We all have our parts to play," came her response. Hitching up her skirts, she guided me up the back wooden stairs into the building she called her home. One glance inside told me everything I needed to know. This was far from the kind of "home" I was accustomed to, and more like the establishment I'd assumed it to be.

Everywhere I turned were half-dressed women being intimate with gentlemen. Some were leaning in close, engaged in sordid conversations that made them blush. Even more disturbing were the few who had hands up their skirts, their heads tipped back in fake delight.

"He left me here in a whorehouse!" I exclaimed in shock. My eyes grew as wide as saucers. Soon other sounds filled my ears—a different kind of music than the piano. I started to back away to the door, careful not to touch anything.

"Things are not what they seem, child." I expected Mrs. Webster to be offended by my disgust, but instead she looked quite proud. "You'll learn that quickly here."

I shook my head back and forth. I squeaked out loud as I bumped into a very large, extremely jovial man. His arms shot around me, and he bellowed in excitement over catching me.

"A new girl!" the drunk gentleman called out, his fingers splayed across my waist. It didn't matter that I hadn't bathed in weeks and carried the dirt from the road on my clothing. Judging from the way his tongue lolled out of his mouth and how his lecherous lips then pursed into a kiss, he only had one thing on his mind.

Mrs. Webster stepped into action and slapped away his advances while tugging me toward her. "Patience, Mr. Jefferson. This one is not for you."

Before he could pout or argue his case, she called for someone —a young girl in a deep green dress—to bring him something more to drink.

I followed behind her in silence as we crossed through the room and then up the stairs to the second floor. It wasn't until she'd successfully gotten me through a small door at the end of a very long hall that she spoke.

"While you reside here with me, I will protect you, but make no mistake. The life you were once accustomed to is over. The sooner you welcome your new reality, the easier you will adjust." She rattled off a short list of instructions—where I'd be sleeping, the few meager dresses she'd managed to find for me, and eating arrangements, but it all became a blur again as exhaustion took over.

"Will . . ." I couldn't quite finish my most pressing question. All I could do was stare at the door that led back downstairs.

"We'll discuss that in more depth tomorrow. For now, change out of those clothes and get cleaned up. Someone will bring you something to eat shortly, and then I suggest you get some sleep."

"But—"

She shook her head. "Tomorrow."

Mrs. Webster left me standing there alone in the center of the room. As I closed my eyes and took in a deep breath, there was only one thought that anchored me, kept me from floating away.

Find me, Marcus. Find me and bring me home.

CHAPTER 1

MARCUS

1879 – EARLY SUMMER – HAVENWOOD FALLS

I was restless.

After almost a year of traveling over ocean and then land, we'd arrived in the mysterious town whose name Lady Hannah had scribbled across the paper she had delivered. During that time, I'd clung to the message like it was a lifeline that somehow connected me to my Catriona.

That was something that had changed—the way I viewed the young woman I'd once considered a hindrance and nuisance. She was far from that now. She was the only creature I would ever scour the earth for, but as much as I'd kept my hope in finding her alive and strong, the past week had drastically attacked it.

Even now, as I stared at the crumpled piece of parchment, looking down at the memorized words written there, I dreaded having to face reality.

There was a good chance she would remain forever lost.

There was an even more convincing possibility that she hadn't survived the treacherous trip across the seas.

"We'll find her," came the optimistic voice from across the room. "Whether we find her alive or find her grave, we'll discover the truth, Marcus."

So much had changed between me and the young man who had left behind everything to follow me on my most important mission. Once he was simply a means to an end—someone to run my errands and provide me with things I couldn't get for myself.

Phineas Knox was now my brother—blood or not.

Our relationship went beyond his oath to help me break the curse that reduced me to a blood-drinking vampire. He had proven in every way that mattered that he would stand by my side— through thick and thin—and his need for justice ran as deep as my thirst for retribution.

We would find the woman who had secured a place in our hearts. Even if it meant dying in the process.

"The thought of her alone out there with that bastard still makes my blood boil," I answered, letting out a heavy sigh and raking my fingers through my hair. There was no disguising the frustration that had become a permanent part of my voice. Everything irritated me, and because of that, my hunger constantly tugged at me. Knox did his best to help assuage the more beastly parts of my nature, but frankly, it was the least of my worries. "Just give me one minute with the Romani scum and I'll be satisfied."

The sentiment was also a steady topic during our daily conversations. While Knox wasn't as bloodthirsty in his plans for revenge, I knew that once this journey came to an end, the thief wouldn't be identifiable—even to the closest of his kin.

I finally put down the note. Staring at it always left an angry, bitter taste in my mouth and a tight feeling in my chest.

Helplessness wasn't an emotion I tolerated, yet that's exactly what I'd been reduced to, and it rankled.

My fist slammed down hard on the desk. "She has to be here." Knox approached, rolling up his sleeve. I shook my head in strong refusal. "No. It's too soon."

Being new to Havenwood Falls, we still hadn't located a fresh blood source, and Knox had decided that he would be my willing donor until something surfaced. We were both extremely cautious not to draw attention to ourselves, ensuring that nothing prevented our moving freely from town to town.

Catriona was our priority.

My bloodlust had to be managed, but even now I pushed down the hunger that gnawed away inside me.

"Just enough to take the edge off, Marcus." And with that, he shoved his bare wrist in my face. "Quit being a stubborn arse and take what you need." When I continued to refuse, Knox finally grabbed me by the shirt and dragged me in front of the bronze-framed mirror hanging on the wall. Whisper Falls Inn had comfortable enough accommodations, and while it paled in comparison to Smithersby Field, it met our needs. "Unless you'd like to take up Madame Luiza's offer and have her bring bottled blood to you. There's also the den. You decide."

I hated being reliant on anyone. It was bad enough that I needed Knox in order to survive and not reveal my vampiric nature. Despite being told that arrangement could be made for me, I was hesitant to become indebted to this town and the citizens living here.

I stared into the mirror and saw more evidence that I needed to drink.

The reflection staring back at me looked like a man dancing precariously along the edge of mania. My long hair was tousled from my constant pulling at it in annoyance, and the sunken expression around my eyes spoke of the countless nights when sleep had evaded me.

"You look like shit," Knox commented. There was no humor in his tone. He knew exactly how dangerous I was when my thirst was left unchecked. We'd had to flee a few towns along the eastern coast of America because I'd foolishly overestimated my own strength. The last thing I wanted was to leave a trail of dead bodies behind us.

I finally nodded, submitting to his common sense. "We need to find her, Phineas." I repeated my desire again before pressing my lips to the pulse at his wrist. I closed my eyes and pictured her face. "I can't lose her."

My fangs dropped instantly, and with gentle care, I slipped them into his flesh. That first drop of blood hit my tongue like a lightning bolt, zinging power and electricity through my veins. It was the same each and every time I tasted blood. Hunger exploded within my chest, and I fought to keep the temptation to gorge myself in check.

Knox placed his hand at the back of my head when I tried to pull away, resisting the urge to take more. He was another one who often overestimated his limits, making us quite the pair. There was nothing more terrifying than realizing how closely I had brought him to death. I'd made that mistake twice and vowed never to let it happen again.

What I didn't confess out loud was I would've rather drained some stranger in an alley than kill the only man I considered my brother. He was the one who kept me human during this past year.

I wouldn't repay him by being greedy.

My teeth slid back in, and I began my count to ten. Just ten seconds, and that would need to be enough.

There was something intimate between us whenever blood was

exchanged. It deepened the love that I had for Knox. It produced a level of gratitude I'd never experienced before.

When I pulled back a second time, he didn't stop me. Instead he simply sat there beside me with his eyes closed, a slight sheen of sweat across his forehead.

"Did I take too much?" I asked, already knowing his response. It was always the same.

He shook his head and raised a shaking hand to his mouth, wiping softly across his lips. A trickle of blood streamed from the two bites at his wrist, and I swiftly took hold of his arm and brushed my tongue across the wounds. Within seconds, any hint of what I'd just done was gone.

"You took what I freely gave, Marcus." I didn't like the quiver in his voice. I hated how weak it made him sound—how weak I'd made him.

"No more, you hear me?" I countered firmly. With each breath I took, I grew stronger as his life force swept through my entire body. I didn't need to peer in the mirror again to know that vibrancy had returned to my features. The guilt that always followed feeding from Knox fueled my need to break this curse.

I didn't want to be the monster anymore.

I didn't want to hurt those I loved.

Knox's eyelids fluttered open, and he gave me a sidelong glance. "This is the safest way, and you know it."

There was a slight hint of red returning to his cheeks, but not enough to stem my worry.

"No more," I repeated. Leaving him to sit by himself, I gathered up a plate of leftovers from last night's meal and brought it to him. "I won't risk you again, Knox, and that's the end of it. Look me in the eyes and tell me that it's not taking a toll on you."

He took the plate from me and slowly broke off a piece of stale bread. Knox took a bite before tossing it back with the rest of his meal. "At least let me find an alternative, Marcus. Please. I need to find more ingredients for your daily elixir as well. Perhaps Havenwood Falls has something available for people like us."

That had definitely been a surprise. Not only had Lady Hannah's message led us far from home, but it had brought us to a small, newly established town where supernatural creatures like me lived amongst humans. From what we'd been able to discover, they lived in relative peace, following the rules that the governing council enforced.

"Don't you think Saundra Beaumont would've told us that when we met with her?" I answered, going over that brief meeting in my mind.

While a man called Roman Bishop had met us and led us into town a week ago, it was a young witch who had approached us the next day and provided an introduction and small tour. There weren't many instructions other than the obvious—don't stand out and don't cause trouble. We in turn shared our intentions and what had brought us to Havenwood Falls. Miss Beaumont had patiently listened to our ordeal and offered some suggestions about searching for Catriona. She was especially intrigued—and seemed none too pleased—that a seer all the way in London had revealed the existence of her secret town.

When we parted ways, it was with the promise that she would ask her own questions and perhaps shed more light on my wife's whereabouts. As a witch, she had access to a coven, and no amount of begging and bribery from me could convince her to allow me to be there when she did.

"Things are done differently here," she'd added before excusing herself.

It wasn't until Knox had convinced me that we needed to play by the rules and not storm the keep, so to speak, that I calmed down and accepted that there were things beyond my control.

I would be nice and polite.

I would nod and smile, if needed.

But my patience was wearing thin.

I needed something—anything—some kind of news to hold on to.

Jumping up, I paced back and forth before striding over to the window to peer out. It was still somewhat early in the morning, and the streets were only now starting to get busy. All I could think of was that someone out there held the information I desperately needed. "Eat more and then go run your errands. I need time to think."

"I'd prefer we go out together," came his reply. Knox sounded stronger, and sure enough, his skin had returned to its usual color. A few more meals beneath his belt and he'd be back to normal.

"I don't need babysitting. Contrary to your false assumptions, I am quite capable of looking after myself." My response came out harsher than I intended. The room fell silent as I felt him measure my words. "Knox," I added curtly, "I won't be coddled."

I saw the exact moment when he relented. With a brisk nod, his gaze returned to his plate as he polished off the remaining food.

"Be careful," Knox answered after swallowing the last mouthful of his meal.

Peeking through the curtains again, I gazed up at the sky. It was another bright, sunny summer day, and my eyes trailed up to where the mountain peaks stood tall and proud. "Perhaps we should go exploring. The gypsy may have her camping out there in the wilderness somewhere. That may be why we haven't found her here in town."

"I'll gather provisions, then."

Suddenly I needed to be out in the fresh air, and not breathing in the staleness of the room. "Good."

With a quick farewell, I closed the door behind me and made

my way toward the stairs leading down. In my haste to get out, I bumped into the small human woman responsible for cleaning the rooms.

"Sorry, sir," she exclaimed, ducking her head apologetically. "I didn't see you there."

Steadying her, I offered a smile that said no harm was done. It triggered a thought. "Do you mind if I ask you a question?"

Her stricken expression turned into one that was willing to help. "Of course." Her blue eyes brimmed with eagerness. "How can I assist?"

"If I wanted to find something here in town but I didn't know who best to ask, where would you suggest I go?" When her brow furrowed in concentration, I added more to clarify what I needed. "Is there someone I could talk to that knows things about the town?"

That appeared to make things much easier, as she nodded excitedly. Looking to see if anyone else was nearby, she leaned in and whispered like we were joint conspirators. "I'm not supposed to know what goes on in there, but everyone does, and it's not really a secret. Just don't tell anyone who told you, because I would get a thrashing from my father. Respectable folks don't go there."

Her response intrigued me. "This will be between you and me. You have my word as a gentleman."

That elicited a giggle from her.

"You need to talk to Mrs. Fanny Webster." She said it as if the name should spark some kind of recognition. I'd never heard it before, and my face must've reflected that, because in an even softer whisper the young maid continued. "She runs the whorehouse here in town."

It was my turn to laugh.

Of course. If there was one truth that was universal in this world, it was that loose morals led to looser lips, and many a secret was spilled in such establishments where liquor flowed freely and legs were spread for money.

"Mrs. Fanny Webster," I repeated, making sure I understood her perfectly. I had. "You have done me a great service this morning, Miss." Kissing the back of her hand like she was one of England's finest ladies in the peerage, I bowed deeply and continued on my way.

I was about to visit my first whorehouse.

Perhaps this journey hadn't led to a dead end after all.

CHAPTER 2

*M*rs. Fanny Webster was not what I expected.

Standing there on the front porch of her establishment, she gently stroked a black raven, whispering something to the creature before it spread its inky wings and took to the sky.

Dressed in a bold red dress that practically screamed her profession, she was far from the coarse imagery I'd held in my mind. I had assumed I would find someone old and weathered by years dedicated to debauchery and boozing, and instead she was a dark-haired enchantress.

As she extended her hand gracefully to me, I honored the gesture with a soft kiss and smile.

"They tell me if there are answers to be found in Havenwood Falls—secrets to uncover—that you are the lady to talk to." I didn't bother beating around the bush or playing along with the charade of false intentions. I wasn't here to bury myself between the legs of one of her girls.

Unfortunately, she felt she knew better.

"Sooner or later they all come looking for me, Mr. St. James."

There was a sultry tone to her voice and in the way she peered at me through her eyelashes. "So, tell me, what kind of pleasure do you seek?" She took her hand back and placed it delicately over her stomach. "Or would you rather I guess? I've been doing this for a while, and I pride myself in knowing what's best for my clients."

Before I could answer, Mrs. Webster placed her finger over my lips, briefly silencing me. With a swish of her skirts, she sashayed around me with a smirk slowly curling the edges of her mouth. "Oh, yes."

"Is this really necessary?" I muttered beneath my breath. That earned me a disappointed glance and head shake. "I've come on business."

"As am I," she cooed in return. "May I call you Marcus?" As she threaded her arm through mine and led me to the stairs, she gazed up at the sky. "I believe it's the perfect weather for a walk about town. You know, to discuss business." There was a slight hint of teasing to the last part of her comment.

I let out a sigh and reluctantly nodded. "Then lead the way, madam." The formality drew out a giggle from her. The irony wasn't lost on me either. "And you may call me whatever you'd like."

I already knew this conversation was going to be exhausting. There were so many pretenses to observe when being social, and it was why I preferred to hide away in my home and let Knox deal with people. He had much more patience than I ever did—even before I was cursed. He seemed to understand what was required, and a part of me wished I'd sent him to come talk with this woman.

I didn't have time for foolishness.

We walked in relative silence. It was interesting to see how other town members treated her, especially those wives who knew where their husbands often spent their time. Dagger-like glares didn't seem to faze her, however. With all the dignity of a queen, she simply tipped her head in greeting and continued on.

"Mrs. Webster," I started, when I couldn't bear the quiet a second longer. In my mind, all I could hear was the ticking of a clock signaling time wasted and lost.

She patted my arm affectionately. "Fanny, Marcus. Please. I want us to become good friends, so let's abandon such politeness."

I'd call her whatever she wanted if it meant she had the information I needed.

"Fine. Fanny."

Her lips slipped into an easy smile. Damn woman.

"My friend and I are here in town searching for someone extremely important to us. Perhaps, with your . . . occupation and talents, you've seen her."

This piqued her interest. "Ahh, so you *have* come to me for a lady. Like I said before, they always do."

The smugness in being correct all but dripped from her words. My tolerance was about to reach its limits.

Counting to ten in my head, I gritted my teeth and faked sincerity. "I'm looking for my wife."

"And you're assuming she's in my employment? I assure you, any of my girls would make a fitting bride for you with the right presentation." All the while, she nodded back and forth with people we passed. She may have run the house of ill repute here in town, but that didn't stop men from calling out her name to bid her good morning.

Something tugged at the back of my mind. This woman was out on display. The swishing of her dress skirts was constantly filling the air, and that was when I realized that I was also being watched and studied.

"Enough!" I said, stopping abruptly. "Let me speak plainly with you, Mrs. Webster."

"Fanny," she corrected just as quickly.

"No. We are not friends. I'm in town for a very specific reason, and once I've found the person I'm looking for, my friends and I will be leaving. Forgive me for being rude, but you either have the answers I need, or you don't." I paused long enough to study her face and recognized the shrewd expression in her eyes. I'd been right. This had all been a show and distraction.

"Continue on then, Mr. St. James, although I warn you, despite what you might have heard about me, I'm too busy to be caught up in whatever town gossip is circulating. If your wife has come to Havenwood Falls, you might be better off asking the Court whether they've met her."

So, there was definitely more to this woman than I first judged.

"Court?" I tested. It was one of the rules Miss Beaumont had emphasized—that the human citizens here remained oblivious to my supernatural nature.

"Now who's playing games?" Her eyebrow cocked as she placed a hand on her jutted hip. "You were met by one of the founding members upon arrival. Or have I assessed you incorrectly?" She leveled a brazen glare my way, holding my gaze.

I barked out a laugh.

"So, you're one of us?" I asked, hoping my question would lead to her divulging more information.

"Who I am is my business and not open for discussion. My suggestion still stands, however." Gone was the flirtatious tilt of her head, the softness in her touch, and the batting of her eyelashes. Before me stood a bolder woman, one who had suddenly tired of our conversation. "I leave the Court alone, and they return the favor. I'm sure if you approach them with your questions, they'll be happy to assist you." She cast a quick look over her shoulder to where we'd just walked. "Now if you'll excuse me, I have things to attend to."

I didn't think. I simply acted, reaching out with lightning reflexes, and grabbed her arm. "I'm convinced you're the one to help me. I'm looking for my wife. Her name is Catriona, and she would've been traveling with a filthy . . ." I abruptly stopped mid-sentence and corrected myself. "Excuse me, she was last seen with a man of Romani descent."

Rattling off the description I'd repeated countless times over the past year, I kept my gaze trained on her features for the slightest hint of recognition.

Nothing.

But then again, what did I expect from an actress? Everything about this woman was about putting on a performance and pleasing an audience.

She at least had the decency to pretend to think. "Neither of them sounds familiar, Mr. St. James. I'm sorry, but I don't believe I can help you after all." Without drawing attention, she pulled her arm from my grasp before plastering another fake smile on her face. "But should you change your mind and seek some form of nightly pleasure—"

I didn't let her finish. "I won't." Frustration surfaced in my voice finally.

She held up her hand to keep me from interrupting. "As I was saying, I'm sure some kind of arrangement can be made. Now, if you'll excuse me."

With a hasty half curtsy, she backed away and left me standing on the side of the dusty street. I watched her leave, mulling over our conversation.

All I could think was how quickly the discussion had soured. True, I'd played my part in that by letting my impatience get the better of me. The blood that Knox had graciously supplied me had burned through my system and left me feeling somewhat cranky. Images of Catriona calling out in fear, of her begging for me to find her, were constantly pressed to the front of my mind. Even now I could hear her voice as if it were yesterday—the gut-wrenching scream she'd released as the gypsy rode off into the darkness with her.

That's why I couldn't ignore the nagging feeling that Mrs. Webster hadn't been completely honest with me. It wasn't something I could put my finger on, but I'd learned to trust my gut, and it was churning something fierce right now.

"What are you hiding?" I whispered to no one in particular. Finally turning away, I glanced about the street and let out a tired sigh. Lady Hannah's note had been so very specific. Havenwood Falls in Colorado, USA. There were no ifs or buts, no mistaking her meaning.

We'd only been here for a short time, but deep down, the truth shone brightly. I'd expected to find Catriona easily. I had assumed that we would be greeted by someone and then I'd be reunited with my wife promptly.

What I didn't anticipate was more mystery.

"Good morning, Marcus."

A deep voice broke through my thoughts, and I looked up to see Roman Bishop standing up on the sidewalk.

Burying my emotions and pulling down the guarded façade I wore like an expert, I smiled. "Good morning. This is quite the town you have here."

Pride beamed from his blue eyes. "It's home." It was his turn to glance about, and realizing I was alone, he gestured for me to join him. "Where's your companion today? Did you say his name was Mr. Knox?"

I wanted to laugh because if there was one thing I believed about this man, it was that he wasn't someone likely to forget details. I wouldn't be surprised if he knew exactly where Phineas was and what he was doing.

I humored him anyway. "Yes, my friend's name is Phineas, but I've always called him Knox. He's running a few errands at the moment, so I took advantage of the fine weather and took a stroll."

His next comment confirmed that nothing was his beneath his notice. "I saw you talking with Fanny Webster." Interesting. He didn't use formalities when mentioning her. "I trust that you were able to find what you were looking for?"

There was no holding back the chuckle that rose up from my chest. "If you're wondering whether I inquired after one of her girls, then I'm sorry to disappoint you. My questions for Mrs. Webster were strictly business. Someone suggested she might know something about my wife and the Romani who kidnapped her. That she may have seen them passing through."

"And?"

I dragged my fingers through my hair in annoyance. "Another dead end."

Roman rubbed his fingers across his mouth while looking down the street. "I've given your predicament a lot of thought since we last talked. I've asked around to see if anyone matching the description of your Catriona even briefly stopped in town."

It was my turn to repeat his question. "And?"

"I haven't uncovered anything yet, but don't give up hope. A town like this . . . with our particular citizens . . . Everyone holds their own secrets. It might just be that she hasn't arrived yet. Are you sure that's what your note was referring to?"

I'd shown him the seer's message that first night.

"What other answer would I be seeking? I was told I'd find what I'd been searching for here. That Havenwood Falls held the answer." Hunger started to gnaw at my gut, but I ignored it. I refused to go back and drink more from Knox. He'd already sacrificed enough blood. The curse was my problem, and I'd be the one to find a way to slake my thirst.

Roman caught my gaze and held it. "Have you not considered

that maybe coming here had nothing to do with finding your wife and everything to do with breaking your curse?"

The simplicity of his question struck me like a sharp punch to the gut.

I hadn't considered it. Well, maybe I'd entertained the thought for a second, but I'd dismissed it instantly. When we'd gone to see Lady Hannah in London, it was for the sole purpose of seeing whether she knew of a cure, but once the attack happened, my priorities and thinking shifted. My need for revenge had been surpassed by my longing to have Catriona back in my arms where she belonged. I felt like an idiot now because maybe, just maybe, I'd come here to America while the gypsy had taken her somewhere else. Perhaps up into Scotland or even across the channel to Europe.

The reality that was a likely possibility robbed my breath.

Could we really have been that wrong?

"Damn," Roman uttered. "You didn't."

I scrambled to contain my emotions.

Each conversation Knox and I had replayed in my mind.

Every witness we'd talked to who gave vague accounts of maybe seeing a couple with a woman who matched Catriona's description tumbled about.

I'd been so sure.

But, again, I couldn't start doubting my gut now. If I began to let uncertainty chip away at my convictions, all would be lost. The hope that I held within my heart still flickered valiantly.

"She's here," I answered firmly. "She's here, and I'll find her."

Roman slapped my shoulder and squeezed the top of my arm. "Then, until you learn otherwise, I'll also ask around and see what I can uncover. While I can't promise anything, it's worth trying."

A need to keep searching flared inside me, making it almost impossible to stand still. "I appreciate your help, Mr. Bishop. I'm staying at Whisper Falls Inn, so if you find anything at all, send a message there."

As I walked away, heading in no particular direction, one thought alone reverberated in my head. No matter how hard I tried to bury it, to silence its insistence to be heard, I couldn't deny the truth.

Doubt had taken root.

More than ever, I needed to find Knox.

But most importantly, my hunger demanded immediate attention.

CHAPTER 3

"*Y*ou're quieter than usual."

I grunted. There weren't any words, and I wasn't someone who spoke just for the sake of it. Knox had found me in a state of panic when he returned to our room. With his arms filled with packages, it took him a few moments to figure out what had reduced me to a state of desperation.

I didn't do well with showing weakness, even when it was in front of someone I considered a brother. Walking about the streets had done nothing but set a steady beat inside my head for doubt to drum along with. By the time I returned to the inn, I was ready to tear down the walls and scream to the heavens.

Despite my adamant refusal, Knox sliced at his wrist once again, this time pouring some of his blood into a glass where he mixed it with some of the herbs he'd purchased. The familiar taste of my elixir hit my tongue, and I suppressed a cringe as I sank into the blessed relief it brought.

My bloodlust was satiated once more, and hopefully, now that I'd ingested Knox's concoction, the beast could be appeased for a little longer.

"Do you want to talk about it?" he asked, stepping over the fallen branch that lay across the faint trail we were following. Instead of remaining cooped up inside the room, we'd taken the opportunity to go searching in the woods on the outskirts of town, breathing the fresh mountain air in deeply.

I wasn't much of a nature lover, but even I couldn't deny the almost healing influence it had on my psyche. After walking for a steady ten minutes, my raw nerves had finally stopped throbbing, and I could begin to think clearer once more.

"There's nothing to discuss, Phineas," I answered softly. I kept my eyes trained on the green leaves that hung from the trees around me. I could feel his gaze and knew that he was worried. This morning had definitely rattled me. Rehashing it would be the same as shaking a sleeping bear. Some things were better left alone.

It was his turn to grunt.

I was grateful he didn't push the issue.

"So, did you learn anything today while you were finding the ingredients?" I assumed he had, because he'd been very specific about the direction we were heading in. After packing a few provisions and shoving them into his shoulder bag, we'd begun walking.

Plucking a leaf from the nearby branch and bringing it to his nose, Knox inhaled and then nodded. "Apparently the town often has people entering the box canyon or at least close to the crossroad some twenty-five miles away. The man in the general store said that every so often, travelers would camp out here in a group, only coming in for food and other supplies. He remembered seeing a group of men enter the blacksmith to repair the shoes on their horses. They were chased off when it was revealed they couldn't pay and wanted to barter instead."

That same burning fire that sparked inside me each time I heard tales of gypsies blazed inside me again. My fingers curled up into fists, and a new thirst raged in the pit of my stomach. Vengeance. If I had my way, I would wipe each and every one of them from the face of the earth. While Knox and I had destroyed the clan who'd attacked us back in England, that didn't mean the sole survivor didn't have family everywhere. To me, they were like the bugs that hid beneath rocks—lift up a stone and a million more came fleeing out.

There was no doubt in my mind that the Romani bastard had joined up with others and that we were looking for another clan. The thought didn't bother me at all. The depth of my wrath would take time to avenge, and I wouldn't stop until retribution was finally delivered to those who had done nothing but take from me.

"And they were last seen out here?" My gaze swept back and forth. The sun above pierced through the leafy cover, and I shielded my eyes from the glare. "How long ago, Knox?" When he didn't answer immediately, I repeated my question.

Knox shrugged. "Maybe a month ago. He couldn't quite remember. From what I gather, his memory isn't always the best. In fact, I noticed that about a lot of the people I talked with. They'll begin to tell me what they've seen, then things get vague."

Damn town. "I wouldn't be surprised if that's due to the Court keeping their secrets. Can't have the humans asking too many questions and discovering that they're bumping shoulders every day with freaks and monsters."

"I resent that comment, you ass," Knox exclaimed, punching my arm. "I'm not the freak here."

I rolled my eyes. "So, you think you're the monster? You hiding something from me, brother?"

I knew this man like I knew myself, and there was nothing monstrous about him.

"Truth be told, I consider you both freak and monster. You'd be lost without me."

He gave me a look that all but challenged me to contradict him.

"No offense, but you're the one leading this expedition, and I'm pretty sure we're lost, so what does that say about you now?" Our bantering back and forth did a lot to ease the tension I still felt in my body.

Knox suddenly stopped and held his head, shaking it briskly as if to dislodge something. "I don't know . . . I can't remember." With wide eyes that couldn't hide his twinkle of merriment, he stepped back with his hand pressed against his chest. "Who are you? Where am I?"

"I rest my case. You, Phineas Knox, are a freak, and nothing you can ever say will convince me otherwise." I shoved him hard as he laughed. "Idiot."

"Sorry, I couldn't resist," he joked. It was good to laugh together.

We started walking again, foliage crunching beneath our footsteps. I imagined that during the winter, everything would be buried under a thick layer of snow. The thought sent a pang of homesickness for Smithersby Field through me. For what felt like the millionth time since leaving England, I wished we were on our way home.

Knox pulled out a folded piece of paper from his pocket and studied it again. "From what I could learn, one of the popular places for the clans to stop is in a glen just up ahead. It gives them some privacy and is somewhat close enough for them to go into town and be back before nightfall. That way they're not leaving their womenfolk alone to ward off predators."

A predator like me, I silently mused.

"Did anyone recognize the description of Catriona?" It was the same question I asked every time Knox ran errands. Wherever we were, he spread the word that we were searching for a beloved family member who'd been violently stolen from her husband. We'd received a few leads, but they didn't ever pan out.

I was starting to believe these gypsies were demons or the very Devil himself. Their ability to keep hidden from me was infuriating

"Just the same vagueness. He thought he remembered seeing a beautiful young woman with dark hair, but then the details got fuzzy." I was clearly not the only one frustrated as Knox kicked at the stone, watching it bounce a few times before disappearing into a bush.

"I'll take it," I chimed in. What I didn't add was I used the tidbit of information as a shield against my doubt. If someone thought they saw Catriona here, I would believe it until shown otherwise.

I was changing.

Gone was the arrogant monster persona that I'd enshrouded myself with. As each day passed, I felt that façade break away, and in its place stood a man who felt vulnerable and uncomfortably exposed. It scared me. When that moment arrived, and it came time to exact my revenge and destroy those who had cursed me, I wondered whether I'd have the commitment to follow through.

Would I falter?

Could I do what needed to be done?

Would I unleash the beast that raged and frothed in the depths of my being, or would I buckle beneath the weight of my reemerging humanity?

"Knox?" I asked, keeping my eyes ahead on the path. I was about to do something foolish again. Damn the bloody emotions that begged for a voice.

"Marcus?" he quipped back.

"Have I changed?" Shit, what a loaded question.

I'd taken him by surprise, judging from the way his step briefly faltered. He hadn't expected me to get so personal.

"Can I answer honestly, or is this a trick question where you remind me who the master is?" From the corner of my eye, I could see him staring, trying to judge my mood. I was tempted to tell him if he figured that out, he'd need to let me know as well, because I was clueless.

"I haven't been your master for over a year now, Knox, and you're fully aware of that fact." When he didn't respond, I threw caution to the wind, and looked over at him. Sure enough, he was smiling at me, and I instantly regretted opening my mouth. "Forget I asked."

Stomping off in the lead, I took in a deep breath and silently chided myself for giving in to softness. Who cared if I'd changed or not? When the time came, and it would come, I would do whatever was required. Even if that meant making it rain the blood of my most hated enemies, I wouldn't stop until it was over.

Before Knox could catch up, we were suddenly in a clearing, and a shot of adrenaline pulsed through me, followed closely by one of disappointment.

We'd found the glen Knox had heard about, and it was completely empty. Signs of people being there—abandoned campfires, tree stumps that may have been used as a table surface or makeshift chairs, and caravan tracks still marked the ground, but that was it. As I walked about, kicking at a few forgotten cups and bottles, I let out a shout of pure anger and shook my fist at the sky.

"For once, couldn't luck be on our side?" I dropped to my knees, burying my face in my hands. The endless searching, months of traveling, vague descriptions, and possible leads threatened to break me completely. I was tired of having my hope constantly challenged and attacked.

That was when my rage turned into something deeper. The stronger emotion seethed inside me and ravaged my soul. Catriona was lost. It was time to finally face the truth and accept it.

"Don't give up," Knox said softly behind me. It pained me to hear his own hope dwindling. "As long as there is breath in our bodies, we will search until we find her."

"I can't do this anymore," I countered, and damn it all to hell, but tears began to fill my eyes. I was splitting apart. The man Catriona believed me to be—needed me to be—was dying a slow death here in the empty glen. "I have surely killed her."

That's what hurt the most. Had it not been for my pride and cruelty, Catriona would be safely tucked away in some other man's home. She would never have become mine, a piece of property to exchange because of financial debt. I should've taken her father's estate—anything other than the young girl who dreamed of love and happiness. What had I given her but a life of misery and loneliness? Now, because of my relentless need to avenge wrongdoings, she was most likely dead.

I felt Knox's hand on my shoulder, and instead of shrugging it away, I took comfort in it. I didn't deserve his pity and compassion, but I accepted it anyway. Like the selfish monster I was, I took and took without any thought of the consequence. How long would it be before I ruined Phineas as well?

"Leave me," I demanded. Bitterness coated my tongue. Self-loathing filled my words. "Go and never look back. I will be your destruction. The gypsies were right. I am nothing but blood and damnation to all who cross my path."

A sob rose up and formed a large lump in my throat. There was no swallowing it, and in my mind, I willed myself to choke on it. I silently begged for the ground to open up and consume me. I prayed that God would strike me down and incinerate me to ash. It was what I deserved.

"Yes." That was all Knox said. Just a simple yes.

He knelt beside me, wrapped his arm around my shoulders, and pulled me in. I couldn't remember the last time I'd been embraced

—that someone had held me close for no other reason but to offer me solace. The gesture caused the lump in my throat to move, and the sob finally broke free. Only it wasn't mere tears. The sound came out as an agonized howl.

I cried until there was nothing left.

I wept until there were no more tears to shed.

I grieved for the man I'd been and the life that had been denied him.

I said goodbye to the hope that brought me this far only to leave me shattered.

"You asked me if you'd changed, Marcus, and the answer is yes." His voice was soft, barely above a whisper. There was a stillness in the air around us, and I wondered if he spoke that way because he didn't want to disturb the sense of peace that had somehow replaced my cries of despair. "And before you say anything, there's nothing wrong with changing. We all must evolve and become something different, something more, if we're to survive and become whom we're meant to be."

"So I'm meant to be this pathetic creature?" I asked, staring down at the dirt on my hands. I was still on the ground. "Is my only purpose to inflict pain?"

"I can't tell you what your purpose is, brother, but what I will say is that you're far from pathetic. You've been dealt cruel blows throughout your life, and you've tried to rise above it. You've tried to do the best you could with the knowledge you had."

I let out a strangled laugh at the absurdity. "Are you making excuses for the horrible things I've done, Knox? Because if you are, you're a bigger fool than I am. I have reveled in brutality. I have ripped into those I believed my enemies without thought or remorse."

Anger heated my words. I could feel it burn my cheeks as I spat them out.

"I never said you were a saint. You are far from perfect. Yes, you were a monster. You didn't know any better. Yet here you are. You're searching for the woman you once viewed as beneath your attention. You're feeling anguish at the thought of never seeing her again. The Marcus you once were didn't feel guilt or remorse. You've changed for her. Don't give up and throw that away." He let out a ragged breath, licking his dry lips as he stared at me. "I'm proud of the man you are . . . whether you are the monster or the man or both. Hold on to your hope so one day, you can show Catriona who you are and let her love you completely."

In all the many years we'd been together, I'd never heard Knox talk so passionately or earnestly. Gripping my hand tightly, it was as though he was trying to will me into believing that all was not lost. And despite everything that still churned within me, I felt that spark flicker back to life. The flame of my hope was minuscule, but it was there.

I just hoped it would be enough.

Brushing my sleeved arm across my face, I wiped away the remaining tears and dusted off my pants before standing. The glen was still empty, yet I saw it with fresher, clearer eyes.

"Thank you."

"That's what family is for, Marcus. We stand by each other's side as a light and speak the truth whenever necessary." And because it was the person he was, he couldn't resist adding, "It's also the role of a brother to kick the ass of the other when needed."

"What do we do now?" I asked, the storm that had raged inside my chest now calm.

"You tell me why you are here on my land."

And suddenly, we were no longer alone.

CHAPTER 4

I'd heard talk about Indians when we'd first arrived in America, but this was the first time we'd actually come face to face with one. Despite the declarations of their savage attacks against towns and travelers, there was nothing to suggest the man staring at us with a wide smile on his face had any kind of violent intentions.

Still, Knox stepped in front of me as if to offer protection. One thing we both knew with perfect clarity was that looks could be deceiving. I was a prime example of that. People often saw the handsome façade of a gentleman without knowing the true beast I could be.

I was pretty sure we weren't in danger, so Knox's caution was more out of habit than necessity.

Placing my hand on his shoulder, I greeted the stranger with a smile of my own. "We didn't mean to intrude. We were walking along the trail and discovered this break in the trees. I hope we didn't interrupt you."

The Indian held a piece of rope that was attached to a few dead rabbits that he obviously had trapped and killed. With long dark brown hair that was parted down the middle and into two thick braids, he didn't rush forward to attack or even raise his voice in anger.

He gently placed his catch down on one of the tree stumps and brushed his hand along the side of his buckskin leggings. Once he knew his hand was clean, he held it up in greeting, nodding his head. "You are most welcome to walk amongst the forest and mountains." Pointing to where I assumed Havenwood Falls lay, his gesture was filled with surprising warmth. "I am accustomed to sharing this land with those who live within the town. We leave each other in peace, as I hope you both will also do."

That's when I caught the thinly veiled wariness in his black eyes. Gossip was always circulating about Indian tribes rising up and attacking white settlements. I saw the wisdom in him presenting a friendly demeanor, yet not fully trusting that we would act with civility.

"We mean no harm," Knox added, relaxing enough to soften the tension around us. "My name is Knox, and this is Marcus." He returned a wave of hello.

The man came forward, and I noticed the vest he was wearing. He had added his own decoration to it by sewing on beads, leather strips, and eagle feathers.

With his hand now over his chest, the man's face lit up. "My name is Ehzno."

I repeated his name over in my head, liking the way it sounded. "Pleased to meet you."

We stood there quietly, looking and measuring each other up. I knew I was staring, but I couldn't help it. I wanted to memorize everything about him so when we did find Catriona, I could describe our encounter perfectly for her.

"Do you need help finding your way back to the town?" Ehzno

finally asked, peering up to the sky. "The woods are not safe at night for those who are unfamiliar with its dangers."

Knox beat me to it. "Then why do you live here? Where are your family?"

We both looked about, and sure enough, there wasn't any sign of others approaching and hiding amongst the trees.

"My father gave me my name when I was born. He tells the story of going on a spirit quest when he learned my mother was pregnant. A bear came to him and whispered my name into his ear. Ehzno means the one who walks alone, so when I became a man, I left my tribe to find where the Great Spirit would lead me." He spread his arms wide and turned about in a slow circle. "For a time, this is where I am needed."

I marveled at how open he was with us—two white men he'd come across alone. His voice was soft and clear . . . inviting even. As each moment passed, I became more and more intrigued.

"You don't get lonely?" It was an honest question. While I thrived living as a recluse on my estate, I still had the companionship of Knox to break the long tediousness of the day. I couldn't imagine being isolated from my family. "Do you miss your kin?"

His face revealed the truth. "There are times I miss my tribe, but I carry them here." He touched his chest over his heart. "And I'm not alone. I commune with the earth and the animals that share these mountains. I have everything I need."

I really was impressed. It didn't happen often, but there was something about this man that touched me deeply. His candor gave me an idea. "Maybe you can help us. We are looking for a woman —my wife. She was taken by someone, and we've come from far away to find her."

As I talked, Ehzno kept nodding, his aged face filled with compassion. "And you want to know if I've seen her here."

I hadn't even needed to finish my request.

"We were told to come to Havenwood Falls to find the answers we seek, but so far, we've uncovered nothing. The man she's with generally camps in woods like this instead of in town. It may just be them two, or perhaps they're now in a group." I stepped forward and waved my hand through the air. "They would camp in an area just like this."

Ehzno's brow furrowed. "I have seen these people. They wear colorful clothing, and at night, they fill the air with music and singing." Scratching his head, he let out a long breath. "This woman . . . describe her for me."

Knox and I both began painting a verbal description of Catriona—explaining even the smallest detail and nuance about her. We also spoke of the bastard gypsy, and it was hard to keep the anger out of my voice.

"You love her very much." His eyes watered slightly. "I wish I could tell you I have seen her, my friends, but the Great Spirit whispers to not give up hope. You will find your lost treasure."

Excitement burst inside my chest, and I looked over to Knox to find he was stunned as well. Less than thirty minutes ago, we were in the pits of despair, and I'd been ready to admit defeat. Now I felt like I could walk on air. This man had given us a much-needed gift.

"Thank God," Knox exhaled, grinning like a fool. It demonstrated how much value and trust we placed in Ehzno's declaration that we so easily accepted it as truth. "You have no idea how much that means for us to hear."

It was the Indian's turned to look surprised. "You believe me so freely?" He glanced between us with his eyebrows arched. "These are strange times indeed."

"You have no idea." I laughed in return. "We've learned to never discredit something at first without giving it some thought. The fact that we're standing here, and not in England, where we're from, is a testament to that. We were told to come, and so we did."

Ehzno chuckled, standing with his arms now crossed against his chest, relaxed. "You are both fools or inspired. I believe you are the latter."

"Oh, trust me. I've often questioned my sanity over the past year." My confession was met with more smiles. "But the world we live in has taught us to entertain even the most improbable."

"And sadly, my own world has taught me the opposite. My people are being scattered and forced to abandon their heritage and way of life. There is great sorrow in this land—a pain that won't fade or stop crying to be avenged."

Now there was a sentiment I understood completely. This conversation continued to amaze me.

A warm breeze rippled through the trees around us and with it, the loud caw of a black bird that perched high on a branch. The sound of it made Ehzno suddenly tense, his head cocking as he quietly listened. Something clouded his features—concern—and his entire demeanor altered.

"I will watch out for your wife and leave word in town should I remember anything. Perhaps the animals will share their stories with me." Backing away, he retrieved his collection of rabbits, leaving Knox and me confused over what had just happened.

"Did we say something to offend you?" I blurted out, needing to understand.

To this, he emphatically shook his head. "No." He then pointed up to the branches where a raven sat, watching us from above. "The woods have eyes—ones that have no business being here. I caution you to take care in your search. Not everyone you meet will be your friend."

His cryptic message reminded me of Lady Hannah, the seer we'd tried to meet in London. As much as I appreciated his warning, part of me wished someone would speak plainly with us and expose those trying to deceive us and withhold information. Like a pirate with his cherished treasure map, for once I wanted to look at the note in my pocket and find a large red cross that said, "Here she is. Come get her."

"We appreciate your help, Ehzno. If we can do anything to return your kindness, you need only ask." Knox's sentiment was reinforced with my murmured agreement. We didn't have much, but this Indian had brought us comfort. We were grateful.

Just as we began returning back to the trail that led away, our new friend called out, waving for us to meet him halfway. In his hand was a leather pouch, and he shoved it into mine before curling my fingers around it. "I was a medicine man for my people. You could say I am a shaman. I believe this will help you with your problem."

Loosening the strings and opening the small sack, I showed its contents to Knox. I had no idea what the plant was, and it seemed he didn't either.

"This is burdock root. My people use it to help with hunger and to purify the blood."

My mouth gaped open. "How did you—?" I couldn't even finish my sentence.

Ehzno simply smiled. "You are not like other men, Marcus. You carry your own burden that weighs your spirit down. Partake of this root, and it will ease your hunger." There was so much knowing in his inflection that I didn't bother questioning him to see if he truly realized what afflicted me. "Should you need more, you'll find it growing beside the waterfall. The water there contains great magic. Go in peace."

And before I could thank him again, Ehzno strode away and disappeared into the trees.

"Shit." Knox's utterance reflected my own. "I've seen some

strange things, Marcus. Weird occurrences I couldn't begin to explain, but that . . . that was different."

I bounced the pouch in my hand before giving it over to him. "Do you think it'll help?"

Sniffing the contents, he shrugged. "It's worth a try."

We headed back to town in silence, both of us lost in our own thoughts. Later that night, after he'd brewed the root into a tea, I downed a small cup of it in one mouthful, waiting to see if I felt any effects.

The results were borderline miraculous.

The constant pressure in my gut to feed softened. My thirst for blood didn't feel so overwhelming.

"That must be some water," I exclaimed.

One thing was definitely clear.

There was magic in these mountains.

For the first time in a long time, I was looking forward to tomorrow.

CHAPTER 5

A piercing shriek exploded in the still night air.

Knox had only just fallen asleep when he bolted upright, looking over to where I was sitting by the window. "What the hell was that?"

Instead of answering, I pushed aside the curtains, and to my surprise saw people filing into the streets from their homes and establishments that were still open. I couldn't quite see where the source of screaming had come from, but there was no denying that things were becoming chaotic quickly.

"Something's happened," I finally replied, stating the obvious. "And whatever it is, it sounds like trouble." More and more lanterns were being lit and illuminating the now vacated buildings. At this rate, I was pretty sure that all of Havenwood Falls was awake and seeking answers.

Knox was already getting dressed, pulling on his boots before quickly running his fingers through his tousled hair. "You coming?"

I hadn't moved to join him.

"Is it really any of our business? We don't belong here, Knox, so what kind of help could we possibly offer? If anything, we'd just get in the way, along with every other onlooker." As tempting as it was to join the crowd that I'd seen forming, there was an uneasy feeling in the pit of my stomach. Trouble was brewing, and I wanted no part of it.

"How can we ask for help if we're not willing to extend that same gesture?" He didn't usually show his annoyance over my stubbornness, but tonight he displayed it boldly. "Imagine how differently your life would have been if others had come to your aid that night in the alley?"

I visibly flinched at the sharpness of his tongue. "That was a low blow, Phineas, and you know that." My voice trembled with hurt. "You've been awoken abruptly, so I'm going to blame that on your still being half asleep." Standing up, I walked over to the neglected bed I'd failed to sleep in. There'd been too many thoughts rumbling around in my mind for me to even consider lying down. "You can't go down there alone."

I reluctantly began putting my own shoes on. I was still in my clothes from the day.

"Marcus," he started, contrition entering his voice.

"You're right." I left it at that. The night air was cool, but I didn't bother grabbing my coat. "Let's see what's happening."

Knox reached for my arm as I strode past him toward the door. "I didn't mean to say that, Marcus. I spoke without thinking."

I simply nodded, holding the brass doorknob so he could go into the hallway. Locking the door behind me, I soon discovered we weren't the only ones in the inn to hear the melee and decide to see what the commotion was. The inn's manager, Irina, was standing outside with her hand raised to her eyes like it would somehow help her see better.

"I knew one day that saloon would bring trouble to this town. Drinking and gambling to all hours of the night. Folks stop having common sense the moment the sun goes down. Why they don't all head home to bed is beyond me." She tutted her disapproval, but that instantly changed the moment she saw Knox and me descend the front steps. "Oh, gentlemen. Please forgive the disturbance. Go back up to your room and think no more about this craziness." Madam Petran tried to shoo us away with her hand. Apparently, she wasn't worried in the slightest.

"I'm guessing screaming like a banshee is a common occurrence here?" I ventured, not quite ready to return inside. Now that I was up, my curiosity had been piqued. Knox had been right. If I wanted the help of others in finding Catriona, I couldn't turn my nose up at a chance to offer my own goodwill.

"Listen to me closely. Haven Saloon caters to all kinds of people in town, and that means a lot of hotheaded men with something to prove." As much as she dismissed the commotion, Irina still cast a look or two over her shoulder.

"We're no strangers to drama. Is it normal for a woman's scream to come from the saloon, however?" That was what kept me in the street. I'd been in enough bars at this time of night to know that if a fight broke out, it would be masculine voices disturbing the peace. Hell, we would've heard gunshots fired into the air.

No, something else was creating this scene.

Knox, in an unusual display of impatience, gently took the lady by the elbow and maneuvered her so she didn't block our path. "We appreciate your concern, but neither of us will be able to sleep until we see for ourselves. By all means, let me help you back inside so you're not out in the night air." Before she could argue, he swiftly led her up the stairs, returning within a few moments. "Okay, let's go."

It didn't take long before Madam Petran's theory was proven wrong. The saloon stood empty as everyone had already rushed out, forming a large group outside a familiar building.

It was Mrs. Fanny Webster's bordello.

I broke into a run.

What I found as we finally reached the crowd made me come to a grinding halt, Knox banging into me shortly after.

"Good God." It was the only thing I could utter.

"Shit." That was becoming one of Knox's favorite words.

The scene unfolding before us was like something out of some macabre story, but that wasn't what hit me like I'd been kicked in the chest by a horse. The sight of Mrs. Webster rocking the body of a dead girl in her arms, blood everywhere, instantly transported me out of Havenwood Falls, and immediately dumped me back in my own personal nightmare.

Even the smell was the same—that cloying, coppery scent that permeated through the air and clung to every breath I inhaled. I could taste it. I was suffocated by it. Shaking my head as if to refuse this as real, I stepped back into Knox.

"No," I whispered, my voice ragged with distress. "Not again. Not again."

My friend didn't move but instead drew his arm around me as he leaned in closer. "Compose yourself, Marcus. This is not the time or place to fall apart."

His counsel broke against me, yet the warning didn't touch my thoughts. All I could see was the lifeless body Fanny was gripping tightly. I remembered that rocking motion. I knew without a shadow of a doubt that I wore that same disbelieving, horrified expression that night as well.

I choked on the emotions bubbling in my throat. Without thinking, I began wiping my hands over and over, as if somehow my fingers were coated with the same red ichor and gore.

Someone shook me sharply—one, two, three times. Then as if out of a daze, I finally registered the alarming sounds that filled the night air. The crowd was rapidly becoming a mob, different sections calling for justice over the death of the girl. I didn't want to look too closely, but judging by the clothes she wore, she'd been one of Fanny's workers.

It felt wrong to call her what she was.

Death had all but stripped away the taint of being a whore.

"If you ask me, that's what you get when you make sinning your business!" came a cry, followed closely by more muffled cries of agreement. It shocked me to hear the life of this woman be so callously dismissed

"Where's the sheriff?" came a voice from just in front of me. "Find the bastard before he murders innocent women!"

There was going to be a lynching if order wasn't established again. As I glanced about nervously, not liking the way the dark energy pressed against me as though at any moment the atmosphere would suffocate me, I caught a glimpse of a man staring at me intently.

"Knox," I murmured beneath my breath. "We're being watched." As carefully as I could, I told him where the gentleman was, and sure enough, Knox saw him as well.

"He's looking at us instead of the body."

I'd thought the exact same thing. "I don't like this."

I saw Knox nod from the corner of my eye.

"I'm beginning to think you were right, Marcus. Perhaps we should've left this up to the locals and not gotten involved." He chewed on his bottom lip nervously, shifting his weight between his two feet.

The tension in the crowd continued to grow more volatile.

"What's the chance of us leaving without having that stranger follow us?" I asked, willing myself not to look his way again. The trouble with that is my focus immediately went back to the blood, and I was blasted with a wave of hunger.

Damn, I cursed. Now was not the time for my bloodlust to flare up.

Knox let out a noticeable sigh of relief. "I guess we don't need to worry, because he's no longer there. That teaches us to be paranoid."

Sure enough, the space where the man had been standing was empty. Being triggered by past memories had set my nerves on edge, and the result had me making assumptions.

"Still," I answered, this time a little louder, "I think we should take our leave now before things get even more out of control." Groups of men had begun to form, and guns were being passed about and loaded. "The humans are restless and needing to avenge one of their own." That stirred up a more obvious question. This time I returned to whispering because I didn't want to be overheard. "Speaking of which, I thought the town was governed by people like us. You'd think they'd be here to contain the mayhem. Keep the peace."

Knox murmured he'd thought the same thing.

Slowly taking my eyes away from the distraught Fanny, careful not to lower my gaze to the body again, I gave one last sweeping inspection of the street and started my retreat. What I needed now more than anything was some of the burdock that Ehzno had given me. With the air coated with freshly spilled blood, I needed additional help.

We only made it a few steps away before the man who'd been watching me blocked our retreat.

"Mr. St. James. Mr. Knox. Follow me." He swept his arm to the side, inviting us to join him.

Knox offered his apologies, politely declining the offer. "Could it wait until tomorrow? We're returning to our room at Whisper Falls Inn."

The expression the stranger wore spoke volumes. He wouldn't accept any kind of refusal from us. "The Court wishes to have a conversation with you both." And as if to hurry us along, he added with a firm voice, "Now."

CHAPTER 6

The man remained silent as he escorted us away from the growing crowd and back through the town's streets. After introducing himself as Elsmed Fairchild, and a member of the Court, he remained tight-lipped, refusing to answer any of the questions I fired at him.

His stony expression and ice-cold eyes added to the whole cloak-and-dagger act he was performing, and I wondered if anyone had ever refused to instantly jump with obedience any time Havenwood Falls' most elite clicked their fingers. Knox and I weren't part of their community. As far as we were concerned, the exact second our mission was completed, we were going to get the hell out of this country and back to the comfort and familiarity of home.

Where others viewed this new land as a place of freedom and opportunity, all it did was remind me how alone and out of place I felt. I enjoyed the anonymity and being able to leave the estate without a hundred tongues wagging with gossip, but not enough to abandon the ease and wealth I'd grown up with.

I knew my place back in Suffolk County—recluse or not.

"Can you at least inform us why we're being summoned?" I asked, trying again to elicit some kind of response. "Does your Court usually hold these secret sessions in the middle of the night?"

Knox cleared his throat beside me, ever the diplomat. I could almost hear him begging me to stop and not aggravate the situation. I didn't care if my anger spoke against me. As far as I was concerned, neither of us had done anything wrong, and their time would be better spent trying to catch the killer who had struck after dark.

"Are you worried, Mr. St. James?" He sounded calm, bored even, like this was something he did on a regular basis.

"Should I be?" I fired back with enough heat that it caused the man's lips to slightly turn upward. Whatever he was thinking, he kept it to himself. His lack of conversation was infuriating.

"Marcus, please," Knox chided as he grabbed hold of my wrist, making me stop for a second. "We don't know why this meeting has been called, so how about we not jump to conclusions before they provide an explanation. They may be needing our help."

He was the optimist to my pessimist.

Mr. Fairchild made a noise that sounded a lot like a suppressed laugh. "I assure you, we are quite self-sufficient, gentlemen." As we reached a darkened home, he approached the wooden door and opened it quickly. "After you." The wave of his hand did little to soothe my agitation.

I shook my head. "No, after you." Childish or not, there was no way I was walking into an ambush. If he wanted us to meet with the Court, we'd do so following him in. "Please."

He didn't miss a beat. "As you wish."

Knox went in after him, but not before throwing me a pleading look. I knew he was just as concerned as I was, but the man trusted too easily. Experience had taught me time and time again that when people weren't upfront with their intentions, it usually meant there was a hidden agenda.

A thin line of light shone through the crack at the bottom of a door toward the back of the hallway we entered. It was pointless to look about and try to gain my bearings, because whoever owned this building had kept it in shadow. Voices started to reach us, setting my nerves on edge again. I had a bad feeling about this.

"Bring them in, Elsmed," a female voice called out, one I recognized. Sure enough, we found Saundra Beaumont and another man standing close together inside the official-looking room. With chairs and tables arranged neatly inside, it appeared like this was where they conducted their town business.

"Mr. St. James. Mr. Knox," she greeted, striding forward to shake both our hands. "Allow me to introduce Raffaele Augustine to you both. He is from one of Havenwood Falls' founding families and holds a seat on the Court. He'll be joining us for our conversation tonight, along with Mihail Petran, whom you already know from the inn."

I studied the other man, trying to get a feel for who he was, but there was no penetrating his blank expression. He caught my gaze and held it briefly. He was studying me just as openly as I was him.

Needing a break from the intense scrutiny, I nodded my head to Mihail. I didn't know whether it was a comfort or not to see a familiar face amongst the group. Mr. Petran had been the one to approach us at the inn about my need for blood.

Taking a page from Knox's book of manners, I chose to change tactics. "Good evening, Miss Beaumont. You seem to have both me and my friend at a disadvantage. Your fellow Court member forgot an important piece of information when he invited us both to this discussion."

She cast Mr. Fairchild an amused glance. "Is that so?"

He simply shrugged and took one of the chairs at the long wooden table.

"We don't know why we're here," Knox interjected. "We heard the commotion earlier and went to investigate. It was in the crowd that he ordered us to follow."

Like a hostess at a fancy soiree, Miss Beaumont directed us to each take a seat, and it became crystal clear that this wasn't merely a talk, but an interrogation. The three of them sat behind one table, and Knox and I behind the other. It left me with the impression that we were appearing before a judge in court.

I didn't hesitate in bringing my observation up.

"Are we being accused of something?" I asked as I perched on the edge of my seat. This wasn't some casual meeting at all, and I wouldn't allow them to lull me into believing this was anything but friendly.

"Do you have a guilty conscience, Mr. St. James?" Mr. Augustine questioned, watching me closely. He was a handsome man, yet there wasn't a smile or glimpse of affability in his features. If anything, I saw suspicion and annoyance in his clear eyes.

Before I could speak, Knox once again put his hand on my arm. He did that a lot, especially when he wanted me to exercise caution. Now was not the time for my sarcasm and temper to take center stage.

"We're only confused over the nature of this meeting. We would've gladly come in the morning and answered whatever questions you might have." Knox offered them all an open smile that seemed to break the tension I'd created. "We have nothing to hide. I feel we've been honest about why we're here in Havenwood Falls and our intentions."

Mr. Fairchild leaned forward and rested his elbows on the table. "You are a vampire, Mr. St. James." Statement.

I nodded, taking a breath before answering. "A cursed blood

drinker, and again, call me Marcus. Surely we can forgo formalities this late at night." I hoped that reminder would be enough to show him that he hadn't believed us suspicious enough to decline our request to stay at the inn. I tried to relax. "I let Mr. Bishop know that when he met us at the edge of the town's limits. I then repeated that information to you, Saundra, the next day."

She acknowledged the truth with a bob of her head. "You were completely upfront, Marcus, which we appreciate. Hopefully you'll extend that same consideration tonight. As you saw outside, a crime has been committed, and a young woman has lost her life. You can see why we're puzzled."

Her response surprised me. "Actually, I can't. I thought that it would be obvious."

Raffaele cut through the confusion. "Where are you getting your blood? We know that the Petrans have told you where you can go within Havenwood Falls to feed your thirst. We also know you haven't used the blood den's services either."

Was that what this was about? My drinking habits?

Knox raised his hand. "While we've been here in town, Marcus has fed on me. We were told where to find a reliable source, but have declined it for the moment. Back home, I was the one who arranged it and created an elixir for him that helped ease his bloodlust, so Marcus decided to continue using me." He glanced my way, his forehead crinkled. He didn't add anything about the argument we'd had about using the town's supply and how I was loathe to rely on strangers for nourishment. "Again, we've been upfront about it."

The sinking feeling in my gut that had surfaced once we entered the room strengthened into a growing fear. "What are you blaming me for?" And that's when it hit me. With my mouth gaped, I finally sat back in my chair, stunned. "You think I was the one who killed that young woman." Another statement.

"That's insane!" Knox exclaimed. "You can ask Irina of Whisper Falls Inn. We've been in our room all night. We even took our meal upstairs because we were wanting an early evening. Madame Luiza will confirm that."

I looked sharply to Mihail, hoping that he'd speak up in our defense. While I hadn't seen him as frequently at the inn, surely he would be kept abreast of what his guests were doing. He seemed to sense my concern and leaned in toward Saundra, whispering in her ear.

Saundra nodded and glanced down at the parchment she had in front of her. From where we were sitting, it didn't seem to have a lot of writing on it—just a few notes she jotted down with her feathered fountain pen now. "We'll be calling on Irina tomorrow morning to check your alibi, but for now, we'd like you to answer the questions we have."

I could see her lips moving, but the only thing I heard was the pounding of my heart in my ears. This was beginning to feel like history repeating itself. Why was I always in a place where something heinous had happened? More importantly, why did it seem I was always the first one to point a finger at? Those gypsy women had refused to listen to my pleas of innocence that night in the alley. No matter what I said, or how much I wanted them to understand, all they saw was the man who had murdered their kin.

Was the same thing happening here, all these thousands of miles away? Would I be declared guilty, despite knowing that I was blameless of all fault?

"Not again," I murmured to Knox. "Whatever I say won't matter."

"And why's that, Marcus?" Saundra asked. My gaze didn't rest on her; however, it was firmly squared on the man whose piercing eyes had already judged me as guilty. "Are you saying Knox is wrong? Were you not in your room tonight?"

My mouth instantly dried. "We were, but . . ." I hated that I had to say that word. "After my friend had retired for the evening and fallen asleep, I slipped downstairs for some fresh air."

The incredulous look on Knox's face hurt. While I knew he would always back me up and that his loyalty was with me, I'd surprised him with this confession.

"Where did you go?" Elsmed demanded.

"Good God," Knox whispered softly beneath his breath.

Closing my eyes, I willed myself to stay calm. "I merely sat on the inn's front steps and watched the stars appear in the sky." It was the truth, as flimsy as it might appear to the others. "I give you my word, that was all that happened. I was feeling somewhat stifled in the room, and my thoughts were troubling me. Instead of waking Knox, I took a few moments of respite outside. Once I felt better, I rejoined him in our room. He found me there when he awoke to the screaming."

My admission hung dangerously in the air—as though the balance could tip either way. I knew how it sounded, and if they truly wanted to blame me for the murder, this could very well give them the proof they needed. They were strangers to me. They owed me no allegiance. All I could do was trust that my word was enough, or that someone else would come forward with the criminal's real identity.

"I still find it hard to believe that someone of your nature could be satisfied with such a limited blood supply. I've known many kinds of vampires, and having only just met you, there's no denying the fact that Mr. Knox is beginning to look somewhat depleted." Relief coursed through me that Raffaele didn't instantly point his finger in accusation and declare me guilty.

He was trying to understand. I could work with that. There was still a chance of convincing them I wasn't their villain. All this time of playing the monster, and now that one had been released in Havenwood Falls, I was desperate not to be viewed that way.

"I'm quite comfortable with the arrangement I have," I answered, not caring that it was a lie. I'd already resigned myself to using the blood den once this fiasco was over, but I didn't want to let them know they were right.

There was no reading Saundra's expression. "So your conversation with Mrs. Webster wasn't about making arrangements to feed while you were here in Havenwood Falls?" She held her pen poised over the paper, waiting for my answer.

I didn't bother hiding my confusion. "What does she have to do with this?"

The three of them glanced at each other, bewildered. The more this meeting continued, the more it felt like vital pieces of information were missing. "She owns the town's blood den."

I shook my head. "No. She's a human who runs the whorehouse. I was told to approach her and see if she'd heard anything about my missing wife and her kidnapper. While I trust that you and your Court were upfront with what you knew, I also know with her clients and business, Fanny Webster might've heard a different kind of gossip."

The spark of understanding I saw sweeping across all of their faces caused me to exhale in relief. A missing puzzle piece had just been revealed.

"She provides both blood and other pleasures to the town members here, Marcus. The assumption was made when you were sighted talking with her that you were making plans to visit later that day."

The atmosphere in the room lightened some more. The air didn't feel as suffocating and oppressive as before.

"Surely Roman Bishop told you about our conversation, then?" When they didn't acknowledge it, I continued. What a mess. "He approached me afterward, and I explained why I'd been seen with her. He'd assumed differently, however, that I was after the other pursuits with her girls."

I looked at each of them, hoping to see that they believed me. I had nothing to hide. With our search for Catriona still going, I wouldn't do anything to jeopardize our finding her. My days of leaving a trail of bodies in my wake were behind me.

Saundra scribbled down something before addressing me again. "We haven't spoken to Roman yet, but I'm sure he'll corroborate your story."

Her comment brushed against my patience and temper. "It is no story. I give you my word that I'm telling you the truth."

"While I'm sure you feel that way, Marcus," Raffaele interjected, his gaze fixed on me, "I hope you can understand why we can't blindly believe you without sufficient evidence. We have a responsibility to the citizens of this town. We must ensure that justice is served."

Hurried footsteps interrupted the proceedings, and before another word was spoken, Roman entered the room. Dark storm clouds thundered in his expression. Whatever news he brought, there was no denying that it didn't bode well.

"Good, you have him. I suggest we end the investigation and arrest Mr. St. James for murder."

I exploded into action, pushing myself from the table and standing up tall. "On what grounds?"

Saundra also stood, and on hearing the latecomer's accusation, thoroughly chastised him for the interruption. "I hope you have a good excuse why you're here, Roman, and not your father. This meeting is for Court members only. Do you need yet another reminder that you weren't invited?"

The stoic man didn't even flinch, his blue eyes boldly holding her gaze. "I have necessary information the Court needs to hear."

Elsmed spoke up again. "And what, pray tell, is that?"

"That Marcus St. James is guilty of the murders." Roman didn't even appear frazzled or repentant over interrupting the discussion. Instead he stood tall, his tanned features strong and unflinching.

Elsmed let out a sigh as he shook his head. "He has an alibi, Roman. One that I'm positive Irina or Luiza can testify to."

Roman continued to stand his ground. He wore a smug expression that told me he was about to deliver a brutal blow to my innocence.

"Then perhaps he can explain why another dead body drained of blood was just found in his room."

CHAPTER 7

*D*amn.

I staggered back in horror, not wanting to accept the revelation that had just been leveled at me. I refused to be blamed for yet another person's death. I couldn't relive the trauma from the past.

"No!" Knox yelled, standing up to join me. While the accusation hadn't involved him, the fact we shared the room at the inn also implicated him in the crime. "I don't know exactly what is happening here, but one thing I know for sure is you're looking at the wrong person. Marcus is innocent."

Roman wasn't having any of his excuses. "Of course you would believe that. How much does he pay you to keep his secrets?"

The anger being directed our way was practically palpable.

I knew tempers would be high tonight with everything that had transpired, but this new development had rendered me speechless. The more I opened my mouth to try to provide some kind of answer, the more I resembled a fish out of water. I couldn't speak what I didn't know, and once again words failed me.

"I don't doubt that something sinister is happening here in your town, but I assure you, again, that we are not involved in it. Please. Why would we jeopardize any help you might offer in finding our family member by going on a killing spree? Yes, Marcus is a blood drinker—a vampire as you call him—but he has been one for decades. He is not this sloppy or reckless. You have to believe me." Knox cast me a sidelong glance, his eyes begging me to speak up in defense of myself. "Believe us."

Roman shook his head. As far as he was concerned, the case was closed, and the mystery was solved. The other four had remained silent during the last few moments, and if their expressions were anything to go by, the only one who looked even the slightest bit skeptical was Saundra.

Elsmed was the next to speak. "We will do no such thing, Mr. Knox. We welcomed you into Havenwood Falls and gave you the benefit of the doubt when you promised that neither of you would bring trouble with you. You gave your word that you would honor and obey the rules of this town. You have been found guilty. You have broken your oath."

It was then that I finally found my voice. "A body in our room does not equal guilt, sir."

Roman actually laughed out loud, the sound of it bitter and full of scorn. "Here in America, that most certainly proves your culpability. Before coming here, I questioned others like yourself, and found each had a solid alibi."

Knox's voice was filled with incredulous disbelief. That and his eyebrows were all but raised into his hairline. "Marcus has one as well. Me. I was with him."

Elsmed cleared his throat, drawing our attention back to him. "While you may not have been the one to drain both bodies of blood, you are guilty by association. I agree with Roman. We have found the ones responsible for this despicable lack of control and crime."

Suddenly I felt like the walls were closing in on me. Any hope of convincing this group that we had nothing to do with the deaths had evaporated the second Roman Bishop had entered the room.

"Knox," I uttered, his name coming out like I was being strangled. "Catriona." Yet another obstacle had been placed in front of us, stopping our investigation from continuing.

He nodded in frustration. "How can we prove our innocence?"

"You assume that you can?" Raffaele asked, a look of amazement returning to his face. "I would think the evidence is pretty damning."

"True, but one thing I know is that given time, the truth will always surface." He said it so matter-of-factly. His optimism was showing again, and I didn't have the heart to correct him. I'd faced this same thing before, and once a person had judged you as guilty, the matter was closed in their minds.

As much as I hated to say it, our time in Havenwood Falls had come to an end. It also signaled the conclusion of our search for my wife.

"Allow us to leave, then," I suggested, knowing it was a fool's hope, but I had to try. My need to find Catriona was still a priority, even over clearing my name. If I allowed this Court to detain me and exact false justice for these deaths, I would never be able to see her safe again. "We will leave town and never return."

It was obviously the wrong thing to say.

Saundra's eyes widened. "You will be going nowhere but a jail cell until we figure out what to do with you. You will be sentenced and then punished accordingly."

I wanted to argue.

I wanted to rush forward and flee.

I wanted to attack before they did so.

Instead Knox let out a sigh and nodded. "Very well. We'll surrender ourselves into your custody and trust that the truth will be revealed. Once that happens, we'll discuss the consequences of this meeting."

Roman's back straightened. "What does that mean exactly—consequences?"

There was no sign of weakness or hesitation in Knox's response. "It means you've falsely accused both me and Marcus and that will need to be addressed. The slandering of our reputations and honor can't be ignored."

Roman's jaw tightened significantly, his teeth clenched together, and Raffaele looked as though he was ready to explode into an angry rant.

Thankfully, cooler heads interceded.

Saundra was the next to speak up. "I agree, Mr. Knox. Yet, for the time being, I appreciate your cooperation while we take a moment to regroup and look at all the evidence. I've written down your testimonies, and will personally validate your alibis. Until then, you will need to come peacefully down to the jail cell."

We were all standing now, and before anyone could lay hands on both Knox and me, I held my hands up in surrender. "Fine. We'll comply with your wishes. I have to believe that truth is on our side."

Both Saundra and Mihail walked us down to where they housed their prisoners. For a makeshift prison, it looked comfortable enough, with two bed cots, a table with a basin on it, and a bucket for waste.

"It's just for the night," Knox murmured as we walked inside, the door slamming behind us. Mihail quickly turned the key, locking us in. "We've slept in worse since arriving in this godforsaken country."

We had, but unlike now, we'd still had the freedom to come and go as we pleased.

"Until tomorrow, gentlemen. Try to get some sleep."

The suggestion was practically laughable, but I didn't smile. There was nothing funny about this predicament.

Sitting down on one of the beds, I stared down at my hands, suddenly exhausted beyond anything I'd ever felt before. With the predictability of a well-tuned clock, my hunger reared its ugly head. Once again, I wished that I'd never been cursed, that I'd never walked into that alley with the gypsy girl that caught my eye.

Knox dropped down into the space beside me and offered me his wrist. He never failed to show how observant he was and how well he knew the signs of my encroaching thirst.

"No."

"Drink."

"No."

I could actually hear his teeth grind together in annoyance. "Quit being stubborn, Marcus. It's not going to help our case if you neglect yourself. You need to remain level-headed and in control."

The only thing I wanted right now was to escape reality, even if it was just for a moment.

"No." Getting up, I crossed the small cell to the second cot and lay down—my back to him.

The springs creaked beneath his own weight as silence descended upon us. It wasn't like him to give up so easily, but that just proved how much he really knew me. It wouldn't matter how long I refused him, because eventually, I'd reach for him and his wrist, and take what I needed.

"Try to rest then, Marcus. Something tells me tomorrow won't be any easier."

I grunted in response. When had my life ever been easy?

As I closed my eyes and willed myself to sleep, I took solace in the images that surfaced.

Catriona.

My beautiful, precious Catriona.

CHAPTER 8

The first rays of the new day shone through the high window of our cell. I didn't need to ask if Knox was awake. He'd been unable to fall asleep as well, but instead of talking, we'd simply lain there consumed by our own thoughts.

Over and over, I tried to understand what had happened and how we'd become embroiled in the town's drama. I analyzed my conversation with Fanny Webster, Roman Bishop, with each and every person I'd met since arriving. While I knew I wasn't always the most approachable of people, I couldn't pinpoint the exact moment where my behavior could prove my guilt.

As for Knox, it was absurd that he could be responsible either. He held himself to a higher standard than I did. Yes, he'd been required to perform all manner of duties for me as his master, but his conscience was just as clear as mine.

"I can hear you thinking from over here, Marcus," my brother chimed softly. "I know you view the world with skepticism, but I need you to trust me with this. I refuse to let this stop us from finding her."

I let out a short chuckle. "And how are you going to do that?

We're not exactly in a position of power here. We're completely at the mercy of this town and the Court. If they deem us guilty, we're as good as dead."

That was the other thing that kept rattling around in my brain all night. There was no way they were going to let us go. It didn't matter that we were supernatural. Regardless of our nature, murder was usually punished with death. Execution wasn't just a human response to violence.

"Then we'll escape."

Just once, I wished I could view the world through his less jaded eyes. "Have you tried getting out of this cell?"

I knew he hadn't, but what we hadn't acknowledged was the flicker of magic that emanated from the metal bars that surrounded us. Even if we couldn't feel the magic that buzzed and crackled quietly, we were dealing with witches. They would've taken precautions. We were stuck in here until they came to let us out.

"If you want to wallow in self-pity, Marcus, then by all means find the negative in everything. You can apologize for your lack of faith in me when I find a way out for us." He didn't say it with malice or condemnation. Just with that same resigned tone he used whenever I dragged my feet and didn't instantly join his belief. "I haven't let you down once since meeting you."

Shame filled me. He was right. I might be looking at the situation with my usual bleakness, but I'd forgotten that I wasn't alone in this. Phineas Knox had always stood by my side, and he wouldn't give up without a fight.

The old me—the one that had been ruthless and unbending—wouldn't have either.

It was time to resurrect him—me.

"Then we will face whatever comes today together."

I could hear the smile in his voice. "To the death."

His enthusiastic response had the desired effect. I laughed. "Always so bloody cheery."

There was a bang of a door above us, closely followed by another one opening.

"Someone needs to be." We both fell silent as we heard someone approaching.

It was Roman Bishop who appeared with a key in his hand, an annoyed expression on his face. "Against my recommendation, you two are being brought before the Court again. Just know, one wrong move from either of you, and I won't hesitate. You'll regret the day you ever entered this town."

We didn't reply or ask any of the questions I knew we both had. Instead we retraced our steps from last night and found ourselves back in that room with the chairs and tables.

"Mr. St. James. Mr. Knox." Raffaele addressed us first, and we quickly took our seats again. "We've asked Elsmed to join us again."

I looked at him, wondering what he could possibly say or do that could change our circumstances, especially considering he'd remained quiet throughout most of last night's meeting.

He cleared his throat and looked down at his own set of papers. They were filled with all manner of notes, and another sinking sensation filled me. A black leather pouch lay beside his hand, piquing my curiosity.

"I'm sure you're aware how serious the charges against you are, gentlemen," Elsmed began. He held a no-nonsense tone that matched his demeanor. "I've been up all night going over the evidence we've gathered so far and read the notes Saundra has provided. I have valuable gifts that are needed in this case." He held my gaze, not blinking until I did. "As a fae, I have a talent in knowing when magic has been misused and of reading minds. If you are guilty, I will uncover it." He paused long enough to let those words sink in with full force. If he thought to intimidate me, he'd miscalculated, because I'd zeroed in on the one word that gave me hope.

If.

Elsmed hadn't said when or even that we were.

He'd said if, and the implication was intoxicating.

I nodded with a newfound sense of confidence. "And what have you learned so far?" I asked, careful not to appear overly enthusiastic. "I trust you were able to find the truth in our alibis?" I sat up straight in my seat, my hands folded neatly in front of me on top of the table.

He nodded. "I spoke with both Irina and Luiza Petran earlier, and they assure me that not only were you both in your rooms, but Luiza noticed you slipping outside to briefly sit on the front steps. She had been tempted to come out and join you. You've both made an impression on the inn's cook, with your search for your wife. She was very insistent that once this was all cleared up, the Court needed to step up its efforts in helping you."

The gesture touched me deeply. I hadn't spoken for very long to the lady, only a few exchanged pleasantries as I came and went from the inn. Her compassion was definitely the result of Knox. He must've had conversations with her that I'd missed.

"What about the body found in their room?" Roman asked, glaring at me. "While we can't prove that Marcus killed one of Fanny's girls, no one else had access to their accommodations."

I wasn't upset that he brought it up. If truth be told, I was curious about it too.

"The likelihood that we're dealing with two different crimes with the same method of killing is unlikely, Roman. I'm convinced that whoever it is, they're responsible for all of them," Elsmed interjected.

All of them.

I wasn't the only one that noticed her choice of terms.

"What do you mean by *all*, Elsmed?" Saundra asked urgently. "Were there more we don't know about?"

All I could think was thank God we'd agreed to be locked up for the night. If there had been more deaths, it would be easier to prove our innocence, because we'd been in the custody of the Court.

"There were three other bodies found." The gasp that echoed in the room was loud. The fae had just delivered a devastating blow, and it had sent the Court members reeling.

"Who?" Raffaele asked, his face bleached white from shock.

Elsmed's voice lowered out of respect for the newly departed. "Two more of Fanny's girls, and a human boy." This time the new revelation that blasted through the room included Knox and me. A child. Whoever this person was, the one responsible was truly a monster. Only someone truly evil could ever harm a child. I'd never felt so horrified as I did in that moment.

"Where was he found?" Saundra's body had slumped with the new revelation. Supernatural or human, it didn't matter. This death was the hardest to swallow and accept.

"Up in the glen the gypsies like to use whenever they pass through."

I couldn't help it. I gasped so loud it reverberated in my ears—overwhelming the thoughts now exploding in my head.

"What?" Elsmed pressed, seeing my distress. "What do you know, Mr. St. James?"

All I could do was shake my head as I looked to Knox.

The glen. We had just been there. Right when I thought I could see a light at the end of this nightmare, we were thrown back into chaos.

"Do you think it's him?" I asked Knox, ignoring the others and the way their stares seemed to bore into me. "This can't be a coincidence. Is he here?"

If he was, that could only mean one thing. So was Catriona.

Knox's gaze narrowed as I watched him scramble for an answer. We'd searched everywhere we could think of. We'd talked with people around town. Yet, was there a chance we'd missed or overlooked something—a sign that she'd been here all along?

"I don't know what to think."

Saundra tapped her knuckles on top of the table, drawing our attention back to the room. "Explain yourself. Who are you talking about?"

It was Knox who answered. I was thankful, because I didn't think I could trust myself to speak. All I could focus on was that that bastard had been here all along—evading us.

"We were in that glen yesterday." I knew what it looked like, that by admitting it we added yet another check in the guilty column. There was too much on the line now. We needed to prove our innocence so we could be released. Our search had to be intensified.

When no one spoke up, Knox murmured thank you and continued his explanation. "We were following a lead but came up empty-handed. The clearing was empty." He added extra emphasis on that last word. "Had we found a body there, we would have immediately returned to town and reported it."

"Unless you were the one to kill the poor child," Raffaele retorted. He didn't look like he was convinced about our story.

Finally, Knox replied with equal force and impatience. He'd reached his limit with the continuous accusations. There was only so far he could be pushed before he snapped and dropped all pretense of politeness. "Do you honestly believe we would be this sloppy? I have been with Marcus for decades. I have served him faithfully, which includes finding him blood and cleaning up whatever mess resulted from him losing control. If this was him, don't you think I would've taken the necessary precautions to hide our crime? Honestly. Ask yourself that. Why would I leave bodies out to be found that would implicate him?"

No one said a word. They couldn't. Knox's impassioned speech was filled with undeniable truth. Had I been newly turned, perhaps they could've argued against his logic, but I wasn't.

"You're right," Saundra said, followed quickly by Elsmed who nodded in agreement. Raffaele was somewhat reluctant to show he accepted what he'd heard. Roman flat out shook his head, refusing to even entertain that we'd been wrongly accused.

"That is one of the reasons I am slow to condemn you both," Elsmed confessed. He stood from his chair and, rubbing his hand across his face, revealing his own tiredness, began to pace back and forth. "Can you explain the look of guilt on your face last night when you arrived at the scene outside Mrs. Webster's establishment? You didn't react like someone shocked. I watched you."

It was time to share my secret.

"Because it brought back painful memories." I took a deep breath and committed to retelling my past shame. "I told you that I had been cursed to become a blood drinker by a gypsy clan when I was a young man. What I didn't share was that it was because they'd found me holding the dead, blood-covered body of their kin."

I didn't lower my gaze as I continued relaying the details of that night. I spoke of the horror I felt waking up and finding Primrose, the woman I had snuck into the alleyway with, dead. No matter how hard I had tried to explain my presence there, they had allowed their grief and anger to consume them. It wasn't until I finished my account that I broke eye contact with the Court members.

"So my reaction wasn't one of guilt at being confronted with my recent crimes, but at being taken back to my past . . . memories that continue to haunt me. I did not kill these people. I didn't kill Primrose either." I stared back at Elsmed. "I don't know what I need to do to convince you of my innocence, but if you're going to condemn me because of my past, then do so. I only ask that you not punish Knox. All he has ever done is show loyalty to me. He doesn't deserve whatever consequences I face now."

I could feel Elsmed studying me—weighing what I'd shared with whatever he'd written down on his papers. "I could invade your mind to reveal the truth. I could place you under enchantment that would force you to confess any indiscretion you've done while here. I have methods that would rip what we need out of your mind . . . out of your soul." There was clearly a threat in there.

Without blinking, I nodded. "Then I submit to these spells. Do what you will. I have nothing more to hide."

He tapped his fingers on the table top, peering to each side at the others. They seemed to be waiting to see what his judgment would be. I wondered if it rankled against Roman's better instincts not to be the one with the final say in matters.

"I was visited at dawn by someone I trust implicitly. It was his testimony on your behalf that assured me that you're not the killer we're looking for. Even though what you just shared is concerning, it's not enough to sway my recommendation that you be released."

"Do you mind if we ask whom you talked with?" Knox had straightened in his chair, leaning forward with interest.

Instead of answering us directly, Elsmed turned to the other court members. "You'll agree that this man's word holds a lot of weight." When their faces clouded over with renewed confusion, he finally offered up the mystery person's name. "Ehzno came down from the mountain to share what he believed with me."

Our new friend was the one who had spoken up in my defense.

"The shaman," Saundra whispered, and I could immediately see the change that came over her. Whatever her dealings had been with the Indian, it was enough to remove any doubt casting a shadow in her mind. "Are you sure?"

"Yes. We need to be searching for someone else. In fact, I'd like to talk more with Mr. St. James to see if perhaps these murders are connected to them being here. There's a reason why the killer has targeted these two, or at least used places they've been to dump the bodies."

Freedom was within sight. "Whatever you need, we're both at your disposal."

Elsmed nodded before picking up the leather pouch and handing it over to Saundra.

Miss Beaumont untied the strings and emptied the contents in her hand. "It's with that recommendation that we apologize for whatever inconvenience this has caused you and release you with one condition." Uncurling her fingers to reveal what lay in her palm, Saundra spoke on behalf of the other members. "While you remain in Havenwood Falls, you're to wear these amulets. They've been spelled with protective wardings. Should you have somehow managed to fool us, and you are indeed guilty, these will expose you."

I didn't wait for her to bring them over to where we sat. "If that will give you peace of mind, then we'll wear them."

I'd carry whatever trinket they required if it meant we could leave.

"Then this meeting is concluded. Tread carefully, gentlemen." It was one last warning meant to remind both Knox and me that they'd still be watching us.

More than ever I wanted to leave and head back to England, but not without Catriona. Tucking the amulet beneath my shirt, I took one look at Knox. We were in total agreement.

There was no more time to waste.

If the gypsy was indeed here, his days were numbered.

CHAPTER 9

"*Y*ou're not going to like what I'm about to say."

After returning to the inn and having Madame Luiza show us our new room, Knox and I both took a few moments to catch our breath and come up with a new plan of action. As much as we needed to rest, we agreed that there would be plenty of time to relax once we knew the gypsy wasn't behind last night's reign of terror. Even as we hurried through the streets earlier, the town members were still rattled and up in arms, calling for justice on behalf of the dead.

"When you put it that way, Knox, I probably won't." I chuckled softly and took another long drink from the glass of blood he'd prepared. I resented having to take more from him, especially when he was already weakened. What I wanted more than anything was for him to agree to remain in the room and regain his strength before renewing our search. "You might as well spit it out, then. I might just surprise you."

We were definitely in better spirits. Freedom had that effect on a person.

"You're going to need more blood than I can provide." When I rolled my eyes at him, he smirked and waved me off. "That wasn't the part I meant. You do remember what they said, right? That they have a blood den here in town."

He was right. I didn't like where this was going. It wasn't that I didn't agree with him. It was plain to see the toll multiple feedings were taking on Knox, his coloring slow to return now. I just couldn't quite shake the feeling that it was like hiring a prostitute. It was funny where I chose to draw the line when it came to being a blood drinker. In the beginning, I had no problem going out and taking whatever I needed—from whomever I saw.

Place that source in a brothel, and suddenly it offended my sensibilities.

I mulled over his comment before answering. I hated the thought, but if it was the only way to keep the suspicion off me and the Court from detaining us again, I would swallow my pride and do it.

I slapped my hands on my knees before standing up. If this was what it took, I might as well grab the bull by the horns and take care of it now. "Fine. I'll go, but while I'm gone, you need to eat and try to rest. We both need to be at our best. You're just going to slow me down if you're passing out like a swooning woman."

His only reply was a rude gesture. I deserved it.

One thing I had to admit about Havenwood Falls was that it was beautifully situated with the majestic mountains as a backdrop. There was a crispness to the air as I stepped outside and took an appreciative look about. I could see why the Court wanted to protect the town and safeguard it from danger. I would do everything in my power to shield the citizens from corruption too, if this was mine. No matter which way you gazed, the view was truly breathtaking.

It didn't take me long to find myself once again at the bordello, and unlike before, I wasn't met outside by the owner. She'd kept me from entering the last time, inviting me to join her on a walk, so as I entered the main room now, it took me a few seconds to adjust from the brightness of the day.

Tables were set up throughout, with most of them being used by the girls and their clients. Whiskey was flowing from the long wooden bar along one side of the room—glasses lined up while a worker poured shots for thirsty patrons. The acrid smell of tobacco filled the air. Someone played at the piano that tinkled out a tune. The atmosphere was lively . . . jovial even, for how early it was.

I scanned the merry crowd for Fanny and found her perched on the lap of a large man whose hand rested precariously high on her thigh. I half expected her to slap him or in the very least move his roaming fingers lower, but instead, she tipped back her head and laughed at whatever he whispered in her ear. Judging by the rosiness in the man's cheeks and empty glasses on the table, he'd definitely had his fill of liquor and was now hoping for a little entertainment.

I hated that I needed to be here. Witnessing everyone's frivolity simply reminded me that I couldn't afford such luxuries. There was no way I could lower my guard to this extent—not that it posed any kind of temptation.

Stepping farther into the room, I began to draw attention from those I passed. Murmurs and stares told me everything I needed to know—word had spread that I'd been under suspicion—and it didn't take long before Fanny looked up to see what had caused the disturbance.

She blanched, her face registering shock before making her excuses to the gentleman. His arms wrapped around her waist, pulling her back down into his lap again. A drunken, slobbery kiss quickly followed, and I wasn't the only one who shuddered. Fanny untangled herself from his grasp and hurried toward me, rearranging her clothes before she reached me.

"Mr. St. James," she greeted, finally composed. "What a

surprise. I didn't expect to see you here today." Her gaze rose to the ceiling, and for a split second, I caught a glimpse of apprehension. Maybe she thought I'd come back to kill one of the remaining girls in her employment.

"I wanted to offer my condolences," I began, raising my voice so she could hear me over the noise and chatter. "Is there somewhere we can talk? Perhaps in a quieter room?" I glanced around to the other doors that led to somewhere else in the building. "Unless they're occupied?"

She licked her lips and smoothed down the side of her hair. There really wasn't a reason to do so, because not a strand was out of place. "Umm." She was nervous.

I should've known that this would be the response. While you would never guess that this had been a crime scene last night because it was business as usual now, with no signs of people mourning, I had been the only suspect. Even though I'd been released, there was a good chance this woman didn't agree with the Court's decision.

"I haven't come to make trouble, Mrs. Webster. I understand that this is a tough time for you and your"—I searched for an appropriate word—"workers, but it won't take but a minute."

For a woman who showed nothing but unruffled composure, Fanny fidgeted before my eyes until she nodded. "If you're hoping to take advantage of one of my girls, I'm afraid I can only disappoint you. They've heard that you were believed the killer, and although you were deemed innocent, the news has left them shaken."

This was why I preferred Knox taking care of my needs. It was less complicated than having to navigate society.

"I understand. I'm not here as a client. Well, I am, but it's not what you think. Saundra Beaumont informed me that you also provide—" I stopped long enough to look about and make sure we weren't being overheard. There were still a few pair of eyes watching us keenly, so I leaned forward so I could keep the next part private. "That you also run a blood den here."

She signaled for the man behind the bar to bring us both drinks. I didn't usually drink whiskey, but I knew better than to refuse the gesture. While I took a small sip, the amber liquid burning a path down into my stomach, Fanny downed hers in one gulp.

Liquid courage.

"I do," she finally answered after licking her lips and placing her glass on the table by us. "Will you be needing that service?"

She shuffled slowly on her feet, and I took a step back so there could remain an appropriate amount of space between us. It felt like a dance, and before too long, I found we'd moved closer to the door leading outside.

"Will that be a problem?" Something was off. Something more than just a little anxiety over last night. "They led me to believe that you could help me."

A ray of sunlight fell between us with dust and dirt particles floating in the air. Just as I was about to repeat my question, she smiled. Perhaps the alcohol had taken the needed effect, because I started to see the woman I'd talked with yesterday—that same self-assurance and flirtatious demeanor.

"Sorry, you'll have to forgive my manners. As you can imagine, I have a lot on my mind at the moment." She brushed her fingers over her brow, stirring sympathy within me. "I haven't slept a wink, and it's beginning to take a toll."

All I could do was nod. I understood that sentiment perfectly. "Then I won't keep you. I don't know how long I'll be remaining here in Havenwood Falls, but until then, I need a reliable blood source. I'm willing to pay whatever price you set." Money. It opened so many doors and softened whatever resistance I encountered.

This was no different. "Would you be opposed to having one of my girls visit you at the inn?"

Her request surprised me. "Is there a reason why I couldn't meet her here in one of your rooms?" I didn't know how I felt about inviting the stranger into the room where we slept. "I'm not sure how the Petrans would feel having one of your girls there at the inn."

I could see she saw the sense in my observation, but that didn't deter her. "While I'd usually agree with you, after last night . . . I just think it would be better if we made alternative arrangements. Your presence here has already stirred my clients up."

Annoyance tightened my chest, and it was on the tip of my tongue to remind her that despite what the town's gossips said, I wasn't the one responsible for the recent deaths. I was tempted to thank her for her time and continue feeding from Knox, but that wasn't feasible anymore. I needed Fanny Webster. I needed to swallow my pride and be grateful for her willingness to help.

I surrendered. "If that's what you require, then I'll be happy to meet in my room at the inn." Beggars couldn't be choosers, and there was no other option available. Not if I didn't want to be accused again.

"Very well, then. Are you requiring the service now, or at a later time?" She took another step toward me, forcing me to retreat again. "I'm sure I could have someone ready within the hour."

I couldn't shake the feeling that she was eager to get rid of me. The feeling was mutual. I was tired of the constant stares. "This evening will be fine. Would you like me to pay now or do I give the money to the girl?"

"I'll set up an account for you, and we can discuss payment after your first visit." Glancing over her shoulder to the now impatient gentleman she'd been entertaining, Fanny offered me a fake smile. "Enjoy your day, Mr. St. James. Claire will arrive to your room tonight after sunset."

Knowing that I'd been dismissed, I thanked her for her time and escaped back into the street. The whole situation had been the polar opposite of our first meeting. I could only assume that I'd lost whatever appeal she'd seen in the beginning, and now I had as much charm as a leper.

It didn't bother me.

Other than blood, I had no use for her or her bordello.

"Thank God that's over," I murmured and stepping down into the street, I threw the building one last glance before putting the conversation behind me. That was when something caught my attention from the corner of my eye. It wasn't the movement from one of the top windows, the way the curtains had parted slightly as though a breeze had made the fabric dance.

No, it was the face that peered down—eyes wide, mouth open, hands frantically pounding against the glass window.

I stood there—transfixed, barely able to comprehend what I was seeing. For a second, I wondered if my mind was playing a trick on me, or perhaps I'd just witnessed a ghost. All it took was a few seconds before the truth came crashing down.

I wasn't hallucinating.

Storming back up the steps, I entered the brothel, and instead of trying to catch Fanny's attention again, I raced up the stairs that led to a second floor. I didn't stop as her workers screamed for help and angry clients swore at having their time disrupted. Somewhere in the back of my mind, I could hear people calling for Fanny, and my name being hollered.

I knew what I'd seen, and no one was going to keep me from confirming it.

I pushed each closed door open until I found one that was locked.

"Hello?" I pounded against the frame, hoping that whoever occupied the room would answer. The brass handle jiggled, but that was all. I was left with no other choice but to raise my foot and kick the damn thing down.

"Stand back!" I yelled through the door, and without hesitation, thrust my heel against the door. It flew open, the frame splintering from the force.

I stood there stunned, my chest heaving from exertion.

All this time.

She'd been here.

Catriona.

"Marcus?" she cried, tears streaming down her cheeks. "Is that really you? Am I dreaming?"

I couldn't speak. My mouth opened yet nothing came out. Instead I spread my arms as she came rushing toward me. Even feeling her body pressed against me, all I could do was soak in the fact that it was truly my beautiful wife.

My very *pregnant* wife.

I had found her.

CHAPTER 10

"I must ask you to leave, Mr. St. James." Fanny had the audacity to act as though I were the one trespassing. Behind her, the man serving drinks at the bar stood with a rifle aimed directly at me. "The sheriff has already been summoned."

Fury unlike anything I'd ever felt almost consumed me. This woman—she'd known I was searching for my wife, and all this time had been keeping her locked up in a whorehouse. Shielding Catriona with my body, I kept my eyes on the two in front of me.

"Are you okay?" I asked, hating the way we were being reunited.

"Take me home, please." Her voice broke my heart. I could hear the tears in her plea. When Catriona touched my back, I wanted to whip around and take her back into my arms, never to let her go. "I just want to go home."

"I will, sweetheart," I promised, trying hard to keep my tone soft with her. Who knew what kind of treatment she'd experienced from this woman, let alone the bastard who took her. From the quick look I'd been able to have, she looked well enough, despite being very, very pregnant. I shuddered to think how that had transpired—what kind of liberties were taken with her. "I'm taking you now."

"I'm afraid I can't let you take her, Marcus," came the smug reply from Fanny. "And if you take one more step toward me, I'll have my man here shoot you. It's not as if anyone will mourn your death, and frankly, I'm getting good at blaming you for my crimes."

"So that was your handiwork last night?" I accused, not doubting her bragging for a second. "Let me commend you for your performance. You're quite the actress. No one suspected that you were the one killing your own girls."

Fanny shrugged, her confidence bordering on arrogance. If she truly thought she was safe from the wrath that was steadily eroding any common sense I held, she was mistaken. The man could shoot me as many times as he wanted. I wouldn't stop coming until I'd squeezed the very breath from her lungs.

"Dimitri expected me to get rid of you. I do what I'm told."

Dimitri.

The Romani scum.

"You need to run." My voice was cold and low, filled with unflinching menace. When she didn't budge, I started walking forward. The rifle exploded, but the fool missed. I didn't have to turn around to know that the bullet had become lodged in the wall behind me. Catriona was safe. I would never let her get hurt again.

As Fanny's hired help struggled to reload, I sprang into action, cocking my fist back before throwing it with the full force of my might. Bones crunched beneath the contact, and I reveled in the satisfaction of seeing him drop to the ground like a stone. If she'd expected me to cower at the sight of him, Fanny had been sadly mistaken. The man could've resembled Goliath from the Bible, and I still would've charged in with everything I had.

Her smugness immediately dissolved, and instead of a conceited smirk, Fanny dropped to her knees, begging for mercy. "Please, I didn't know she was your wife. Dimitri threatened to destroy everything I've worked so hard to build for myself here. All I had to do was keep her hidden until he returned for the baby."

I refused to listen. Instead, I kicked out at her, roaring in anger. "Get up! You will answer for your deceit."

When she held her hands up in front of her, I swiped them aside and breached the space between us. I couldn't think straight. All I could see was the face of someone who had deliberately kept me from my wife.

My fingers curled around her slender throat, squeezing just enough to make her panic. I wasn't someone who thought I could ever raise a hand against a woman, but retribution was needed. This bitch knew how to find her co-conspirator, and he was the one I wanted to vent my fury on.

"Please," she gurgled, her face turning a bright red. Tears streamed down over her cheeks. Gone was the enchantress. Fanny was now reduced to a sobbing, pathetic charlatan. "I'll do anything you want. Just please don't hurt me."

"You deserve to be hurt," I thundered. My body trembled from the adrenaline coursing through my veins. It finally made sense why she didn't want me returning here to feed. We had gone for the walk yesterday, not because she wanted to enjoy the fresh air, but because Catriona had been sequestered upstairs. "You deserve to feel how I do . . . what it means to have everything ripped away until you think you'll surely go mad."

All the while, my wife stood behind me, watching. She didn't say a word, not even to calm me down and keep me from killing her captor. It was a testament to what she'd had to endure, that the one who had boldly defied me to protect the prisoner in my dungeon last year had nothing to say now.

My fingers tightened a little more around Fanny's throat, bruising her pale skin. I could hear a commotion down in the main room and knew that the cavalry had arrived to save the poor Mrs. Webster from the madman.

If I was going to do anything, now was the time. If I waited any longer, my chance to exact revenge would be gone.

Leaning in close until she could feel the warmth of my breath on her face, I held her gaze until all she could see was me. "Where is he? Tell me now and you'll live."

"I don't know," she spluttered, panic filling her eyes.

I gripped harder. "Wrong answer. Try again."

Loud footsteps pounded on the floor outside the room. Help was almost here.

"He'll kill me."

I banged her hard against the wall, frustrated with her obstinacy. "I will kill you. It's me you should be afraid of."

Someone came flying into the room, and seeing the chance disappear, I reluctantly let Fanny go, not bothering to catch her as she fell to the carpeted floor.

"Mr. St. James! What is the meaning of this?" It was Mihail Petran who stood beyond the doorway, his gaze sweeping over the room like he couldn't believe he'd caught me in the very act. Whatever he'd been told, I knew my towering over a weeping woman, while another stood terrified behind me, didn't look good or in my favor.

I held my hands up in surrender and backed away from Fanny. I could already see the mottled coloring from where my hand had been at her throat. She was heaving dramatically now that she had an audience, clutching her chest in desperation.

"Thank goodness you're here, Mr. Petran," she prattled, knowing the focus was solely on her. "He came here in such a rage and refused to listen. I was terrified for my life!" Accepting Mihail's extended hand, she stumbled into him, forcing the man to wrap his arms around her. "Please, help me."

The look Mihail leveled at me was brutal.

"Explain yourself," he demanded.

Before I could defend myself, Catriona came forward, her hand curved around her stomach protectively. "If I could, I'd like to answer that, sir."

Fanny sniffled against his chest. "Pay no heed to her. She's simpleminded and easily manipulated. That's why her husband has asked me to care for her. She's prone to fits and fantasies." Finally breaking away from Mihail, Fanny attempted to cross the room to Catriona.

She didn't make it more than a step before I growled low at her —a reminder not to challenge my patience. Now I'd found Catriona, no one would ever come between us again.

Mihail nodded as he grasped hold of Fanny. Kindness now filled his features. He believed Fanny that he was talking with someone who was more child than adult.

"I'm sure you've had quite a shock, Miss," he said gently. His mannerisms were as though he was approaching a small deer that he didn't want to spook. "If you could just come with me." He extended his hand to her. "I'll see that you are returned safely to your husband."

If he thought Catriona was quiet because she was weak and submissive, he was mistaken. Shaking her head, she cleared her throat. Her answer came out loud and crystal clear. "Marcus is my husband. If I go anywhere, it will be with him."

There was so much strength in her words. Whatever shock she had felt, it was quickly being replaced with the same spark and fire that had melted my heart back in England.

She slipped her hand into mine, and the sensation made me want to shout with joy. I had found her. The message from Lady Hannah had been right. Every sacrifice we'd made, every decision that brought us here to Havenwood Falls, had been worth it.

My hope had been rewarded.

Mihail's brow furrowed, and holding Fanny at arm's length now, he looked between us both. "Is this young woman correct? Is Marcus her husband?" She refused to answer him. Even when he threatened to bring her before the Court. "Sooner or later, you're going to have to tell the truth, Mrs. Webster. We've often looked the other way with regard to what happens in this building because you agreed to also host a blood den. If you want to continue to keep the arrangement, you're going to need to explain yourself."

Something had changed within her. While Mihail had addressed Catriona, Fanny had obviously decided what her best course of action was. The smugness had returned. She peered down her nose at the Court member with a haughtiness that bordered on stupid. There was no way she could believe this would end well for her.

"I have only one thing to say." She turned to me, and I wanted to wipe the demented smirk from her face. "Enjoy her while you can. When Dimitri returns—and he's on his way—he will take the child and kill you all. I curse you to never have a day's peace as long as you walk this earth." And with that, she spat at me, uttering a few words in Romani.

"I'll need you to also come with me, Marcus. Bring the young lady with you." Tugging on Fanny again, he held on to her. Catriona was still holding my hand, and as we started following them out, I kissed the back of her hand.

"I can't believe you're really here," she uttered. The light was returning to her eyes, and all I wanted to do was take her back to Knox so he could celebrate with us. "That you found me."

"We haven't stopped looking for you since he rode off with you on that horse." I helped her down the stairs and through the room that had been cleared of patrons. The only people left inside the bordello were the girls who worked for Fanny. Wisely, they kept their distance.

We'd managed to take a few steps into the street before I heard my name being called. Knox came running toward me. Somehow, he'd heard that I'd been involved in something at the brothel and had come to help. I recognized the precise moment when he realized who I was holding hands with.

"How?" he exclaimed as he came to a screeching halt, his gaze darting back and forth in disbelief. "Catriona?"

She dropped my hand and threw her arms around his neck. "Knox!"

He looked at me over her shoulder, a million questions reflected in his face. "How is this even possible? Was she here this whole time?" That's when her condition finally registered. Releasing her, he stared at her stomach. "Marcus?"

I nodded. "We have a lot to discuss, but first the Court is going to want to talk with us." All I could think was as soon as the truth was revealed, we could get the hell out of this town.

My family was back together.

The realization that our search was finally over still hadn't sunk in.

But pulling her into me again, wrapping my arm around her waist . . . that was a start.

I was never going to let her go.

CHAPTER 11

*I*n the end, the Court found Fanny guilty. Locked up in the same cell Knox and I had previously occupied, she was charged with being an accomplice to kidnapping, but most importantly, she was found guilty of murder.

Once the Court apologized again for their mistake, we were free to go. It was like music to my ears, because I couldn't wait to return to the inn, pack up our belongings, and leave immediately. Havenwood Falls would hopefully become a distant memory, and for as long as I lived, I never wanted to step foot in this town again.

Catriona and Knox agreed as well.

We were all eager to put this behind us.

The only problem was that Dimitri was still out there, and Fanny's final words still rang loudly in my mind. He would come for my wife again. Not just her, but the baby she carried. I tried not to think about the fact that he had defiled Catriona, sullying her spirit and body with his filth. There was no mistaking the love that she felt for the babe growing inside her, the longing that filled her voice whenever she mentioned the child.

I didn't have the heart to remind her who the father was. She was painfully aware of that truth. Instead, I vowed to protect her and the infant. I would step forward and be the man she needed me to be. They would want for nothing, and we'd be the family she'd always desired.

"Are you sure you're okay with this, Marcus?" She bit her lip nervously, peeking at me from the corner of her eyes. Every time I'd tried to talk with her and see what was on her mind, she brushed my concern off as her being tired. We seemed to tiptoe around each other while Knox was out settling the accounts and finding us a way to travel safely with her.

"Is that why you've been lost in your thoughts?" I paused amid folding my clothes, dropping them into my open trunk. If she was finally ready to talk about what she'd experienced, I would listen for as long as it took. "What can I say that will show you how I feel?"

This was all my fault. I'd sowed the seeds of doubt when we were first married, nurturing a sea of insecurity concerning where we stood with each other. Of course, she worried that I would feel indifferent still. I wouldn't be surprised if she saw my being here to search for her as merely me retrieving my property.

Self-loathing cut deep like a knife. I would never forgive myself for acting so badly.

"You haven't touched me since we returned to this room. Do I disgust you now that we're alone and away from onlookers?" Catriona stared down at her stomach and ill-fitting clothes. She couldn't see how incredibly beautiful she was to me—what a miracle she was in my mind.

Tears welled in her eyes, threatening to spill over and stain her cheeks.

I blamed myself for them as well.

"Catriona," I started, choking around the emotions that suddenly rose up. "I have so much to explain . . . so many things to make amends for. Please." I reached for her now, hoping that I could convey what I felt through my touch. Careful not to overwhelm her, I took her hand and held it to my chest. "The thought of never finding you again has haunted me this past year."

When she didn't look at me, I tipped her chin up with my finger. Shame filled her gorgeous green eyes now. "I know how you see me, Marcus. I understand the relationship we have, and that all we can ever be is friends. I accepted that back in England." As she tried to place some distance between us, I shook my head, and held her in place.

"Would you believe me if I told you I've realized how much of a fool I was then? That I didn't truly appreciate you and what you meant to me until after you were taken?" I needed her to hear the words I was saying—to feel the way my heart was reflected in each sentiment.

More than anything, I hoped I hadn't damaged what might have been between us, what I hoped could be, because I'd been too afraid to let her close enough to see me—the monster and the man.

"You're not making any sense," she cried, and I could feel her starting to pull away again.

Had I hurt her beyond forgiveness?

Did my following her across the world to bring her home mean nothing compared to my neglect of the past?

"I love you, Catriona," I blurted out, desperate enough to lay myself completely bare before her.

I could see she was struggling to accept what I was saying. Her gaze kept dropping to my mouth as if she expected it to reveal my true intentions. I wasn't lying, though. The second I'd walked into that room at the whorehouse and found her standing there, I'd known it. Love had struck like a blessed revelation, the emotion enmeshed in my soul. For the first time I wasn't afraid to speak my heart.

And now, I felt like I would burst if I kept it trapped inside a second longer. It strengthened me—filling me with a light and peace I hadn't known was possible. This beautiful woman had rocked my world and helped rebuild me into someone much more than I expected.

She'd shown me redemption was within my reach.

"You don't have to say that, Marcus. It's enough that we can still be friends and that I have a home with you and Knox." It was her turn to be stubborn now. I almost burst out laughing at the irony. So many nights she'd stood outside my study, poised to knock on the door. Starved for affection, for any scrap of decency, she'd risked looking like a fool by approaching me.

Now it was my turn to wear my heart on my sleeve and beg. It was my turn to be vulnerable and take the chance of being denied.

Words weren't reaching her.

No matter how hard I tried to find a way to make her understand, she was too guarded to hear what I was saying—to realize that I wanted it all with her. Everything. I didn't care what had happened or what the future would bring, as long as I could stand by her side and face it together.

Cupping her face between my hands, I used my thumb to brush gently across her cheekbone, marveling again that this was real. This wasn't one of many fantasies I'd had, imagining what our reunion would be like. She was flesh and blood, here before me, looking up at me as though I was a mystery she was trying to decipher.

"I love you, Catriona St. James. I am yours completely, if you'll have me. I can't change my actions from the past. All I can do is promise to never make you feel less than the extraordinary woman you are. I want to be your husband, not just your friend. I want to take you in my arms, and never, ever let you go."

I lowered my mouth to hers, our lips barely touching. I could feel the hitch in her breath, the anticipation of what I was going to do next. It was my turn to be uncertain. What if she pushed me away? What if the damage had been done, if the trauma of the past year had scarred her forever, and convinced her she'd rather be alone?

A million thoughts raced through my mind, but only one stuck. Only one was deemed important enough to act on. With one last brush of my thumb across her warm skin, I pressed my mouth over hers.

I kissed her with all the tenderness I could muster.

I pulled her against me and cradled her body with my arms as though she was the most precious gift I had.

My heart thundered in my chest—the sensation loud enough that I was positive she could hear it. Time seemed to stand still as I waited to see how she would respond. Would she melt into my embrace, signaling that she returned my affection, or would she shove me away, offended by my audacity?

I took courage that she'd allowed me to caress her face. She had wanted me once before. This experience had taught me a powerful truth. There was always hope—even if it was the tiniest of flames. If it flickered in the slightest, it could be rekindled into a burning fire.

"This has to be another dream," she whispered, her eyes still closed.

"Trust me, sweetheart. We're awake. This is real." Feathering my lips gently over hers, I ached to deepen our kiss. "Will you have me?"

Her lids opened, and I finally saw the spitfire young woman who had stood in my office that first day, the one who had eagerly returned the kiss I had stolen.

"You came." Just two small words, but they shifted my world—our world—realigning us. She knew this wasn't some illusion and that I meant everything I'd said. "You came."

Catriona gripped the front of my shirt tightly and pulled my mouth back to hers. Any hesitancy evaporated the instant her tongue touched mine. She poured everything into the way her lips moved like she was finally able to take what she wanted—what had been denied her. Her hand wound around my neck, and I felt her rise up on her tiptoes. She wanted to get closer—echoing the need that was swirling inside me.

There was something sweet about the way she tasted, the way she didn't once try to break the seal of our mouths, the way she kept drawing me into her like she was afraid to end the magic between us.

Kissing her stripped away everything that haunted me, that tried to twist me into a bitter version of myself. I knew how cliché that sounded—that a mere taste of a woman could be so transformative—but there was no denying the change that was unfolding. It wasn't that I was becoming a better man. More like I had finally realized exactly what I stood to lose if I didn't abandon my foolishness.

Someone coughed behind me, and I faintly registered that the door to our room had opened. I didn't want to stop, though. I didn't care how indecent this might appear to whoever had joined us. This kiss had been a long time coming—had taken many tears and fears overcome in order to claim it.

"Hello?"

It was Knox who rudely tried to interrupt us, and I made a mental note to throttle him once we were alone. Trying to tune him out didn't work, however. Not because I couldn't but because he wasn't the only one who'd entered our room.

"Do you think we should maybe wait downstairs for them to finish?" The woman's voice sounded like she was pleased to find Catriona and me in such an embrace. "It seems like a shame to interrupt such a . . . passionate reunion." I could almost picture Madame Luiza blushing, her cheeks flushing a pretty pink.

"They have plenty of time to continue this later, I assure you,"

Knox countered, clearing his throat again. "In fact, I'll probably spend the journey home being incredibly nauseated from them celebrating."

Catriona burst into laughter, the sound like music to my ears. I would never tire of hearing it.

"Sorry to embarrass you, Knox. We'll try to keep your sensibilities in mind, okay?" She was teasing him. One glance at Knox, and I could practically hear his joy from across the room. We were both grateful that we'd managed to find her, despite the odds.

"Forgive me, Madame Luiza. It just feels so good to be with my wife again." I didn't bother hiding my pride and happiness. "I'm glad we're able to speak with you before we leave. I wanted to thank you for the kindness you've shown Knox and me while we've been here. It's meant a lot."

Knox looked at me like I'd suddenly sprouted two heads. Usually it was him who shared his appreciation on behalf of us both. He'd just have to get used to it.

Madame Luiza came forward and took my hand in hers. "I was telling this young man that I wish you would stay a little while longer, at least until the baby arrives. The roads aren't always safe to travel on, and I'd hate for you all to get into trouble with no one to come and help." She turned to Catriona, grabbing her hand as well. "I would sleep easier knowing that no more harm comes to you, dear one. The roads can be treacherous at any time of the year. Perhaps waiting until you've all had a chance to recuperate from this ordeal would be better." Looking around the room, she searched for an ally. I didn't like the idea of refusing her, but I was eager to get going.

"I don't mean to offend you, but the sooner we can get home, the sooner we can put all of this behind us. You understand, don't you?" I asked, hoping that she could see why it was so important we didn't linger. I didn't mention that we still had to deal with Dimitri and the threat he still posed to Catriona and the baby. I couldn't shake the feeling that there was no time to waste.

She slowly nodded her head, but not before I caught the look of disappointment. She'd enjoyed the time we'd spent here in the inn. She liked knowing that she could draw Knox into a conversation or that he couldn't get enough of her cooking. I'd heard him more than once threaten to whisk her away back to England because he couldn't bear going back to the food prepared at the estate. If it meant he was happy, I'd even contemplate offering her a job at Smithersby Field. She'd never leave her family here in Havenwood Falls, but a compliment was a compliment, and she positively radiated with pride whenever Knox moaned over each mouthful.

"You must do what's best for your family, Marcus. Family always comes first. You're a good man to remember that." Tapping my cheek affectionately, she stepped back and wiped her hands on the apron she wore. "Just know you'll all be missed."

"Marcus," Catriona interrupted before letting out a gasp of pain. In horror I watched her double over instinctively to protect her stomach. "Something's not right. Something—" Her words were cut off as she screamed out, clutching frantically for my arm to keep her upright.

"Is it the baby?" Madame Luiza asked as she pushed past me. Guiding Catriona over to the bed, she helped my wife sit on the edge. Sweat was already beading along her brow, her eyes scrunched closed as another wave of pain crashed over her.

Catriona nodded quickly. Panting, she looked to me for help, but I stood there totally clueless about what to do next. Even Knox seemed at a loss for words.

"Go," Madame Luiza shooed, waving us away. "Fetch my sister-in-law Irina. Tell her we have a baby to deliver. Quick!" Knox and I hurried out from the room.

"You go, Knox," I said, stopping before I reached the top of the stairway. "I can't leave Catriona alone. Not again. Go get whatever the women need. I'll stay right here and make sure they're not interrupted."

He didn't argue. Instead, he pulled me in for a quick hug before running down the stairs on his new errand.

Our travel plans were put on temporary hold.

There would be no leaving for home just yet.

Glancing up at the ceiling, I offered up a prayer to whomever might be listening.

Keep her safe.

Please.

Don't rip her from me now that I've finally found everything I've ever wanted.

CHAPTER 12

I'd been banished to sit outside on the front steps. Apparently, my constant pacing outside our room was distracting and agitating Catriona further. Not that I was allowed to go inside and talk to her myself or see with my own two eyes that she was okay. At one point I'd pressed my ear up against the door, hoping to hear something that could alleviate my worry. Each time a contraction struck, I could hear Catriona scream out in pain. It was torture not to rush inside.

"Leave her to us, Marcus. She's in good hands." I had no doubt Madame Luiza meant to put me at ease, but nothing seemed to calm the rampant thoughts tumbling in my mind. All I could imagine was the worst. It was then that she stuck her head back through the door and ordered me away for the good of the baby.

Knox hadn't been any help either. He took one look at the furrowed brow and tried to get me to come with him to the waterfall Ehzno had talked about. He wanted to harvest as much of the burdock root as he could for our trip home. Now that we'd be traveling with a baby, we wanted to make sure that my hunger never raged out of control. This child hadn't even entered the world and already was the most important priority of our small family.

We joked back and forth about whether the babe would be a girl or a boy. Despite what I'd once thought—that I could only ever be satisfied by having an heir—all I could focus on and hope was that the child be healthy. I would love the child regardless of how conceived. I would claim my place as parent with a full heart and strive to be the father the child deserved.

A loud squawk of a nearby bird drew my attention from its perch on a branch in front of the inn. An unsettling sensation washed over me. It was a raven. Heaven help me, but it looked exactly like the same creature Knox and I had seen up in the glen the other day. Ehzno's words echoed in my mind—that we were being watched and there was an ill wind blowing in the air.

I didn't fully understand all of the Indian's customs and beliefs, but I didn't forget his expression as he hurried away. I also remembered that Fanny had been whispering to a bird before our first meeting.

This raven had made its presence known, and I couldn't shake the feeling that maybe there was something else at play. I wasn't one to give in to paranoia, but my instinct nagged that I couldn't lower my guard. Something was coming for my family. Perhaps this fowl was being used as a way to spy from a distance without drawing suspicion.

"Shoo," I called out, flapping my hand at the bird. It cocked its head to the side as though it was studying me as hard I was watching it. Looking around for something to throw at it, I stood up instead and rushed toward it. The raven took to the sky, only to settle back on the windowsill outside the room Catriona was in.

Fear sent me running.

I didn't care how I looked as I burst in and surprised everyone. Excusing my interruption, I tried not to notice how exhausted

Catriona looked, how drenched with sweat she was, as she reclined against the pillows propped behind her.

"What's the meaning of this, Mr. St. James?" Irina asked, clearly alarmed that I hadn't warned them before entering. "You can't just rush in here. We need to keep everything calm for your wife. Any stress she experiences can hurt the baby."

I glanced outside to see the raven peering in. I did the only thing I could—I slammed the curtains closed, effectively shutting the blasted creature out.

"My apologies, ladies." I stopped briefly beside the bed and leaned in to kiss Catriona's cheek. "Do you need anything, sweetheart?" Now I was here, I was reluctant to return to my stoop outside.

She forced a smile on her face, even though pain filled her eyes. "I'm okay, Marcus. You don't need to stay with me. The baby and I are fine."

Luiza saw that as her opportunity to move me along. "You can see for yourself that things are progressing. I promise you, I'll fetch you as soon as the infant arrives. Until then, you'll just be under foot and worry your poor wife."

With every step I took toward the door, I felt a weight pulling me back. I didn't care that other men chose not to welcome their child into the world and stay. I'd already missed so much, and I still worried that if Dimitri were to show up, I would be too far away to protect her.

I was abruptly pushed the rest of the way out the door, turning only to have it slammed in my face. Maybe I should've gone with Knox instead of obsessively staring up at the window. Anything had to be better than impatiently waiting.

"How much longer, Madame Luiza?" I called through the wooden door.

"At least a few hours, maybe more." Came her response.

Hours.

I wasn't going to survive this.

Thankfully I wouldn't be pacing the front porch alone, because it wasn't long before Knox came rushing back, his face bursting with excitement. The bag that he'd taken with him to gather the needed root was nowhere to be seen. Whatever was happening had caused him to leave it behind.

"You need to come now." He didn't wait for me to answer. He all but dragged me down the stairs and back in the direction he'd come. As much as I wanted to share in his news, I dug in my heels, bringing his effort to a grinding halt.

"I'm going nowhere, Knox. Not while Catriona needs me." I couldn't believe he'd forgotten why I'd stayed behind. Even now he was trying to get me to move.

"You don't understand. I found it. Lady Hannah was right. The answer to all your problems is here in Havenwood Falls. Ehzno, bless the Indian's heart, showed us where to find it. Hurry up!" he exclaimed fervently. "There's no time to waste."

He wasn't making any sense. We'd both agreed that the seer's message had been referring to Catriona and where the gypsy had taken her. Seeing that prophecy come true, the case was closed in my mind.

"You're not listening. I can't go anywhere right now." I resorted to pointing up to the window where the raven still sat. "Especially not while that blasted thing stays. Recognize anything?" I gestured again, hoping that he would calm down long enough to see it wasn't safe to go on some errand with him.

"Is that the same one?" Finally, Knox was beginning to see reason. Dropping my arm, he sauntered closer, peering up to the ledge. "Do you suspect magic?"

I nodded. "Call me crazy, but I think the gypsy has somehow spelled that raven to spy for him. What better way to keep track of

Catriona and the baby while remaining hidden? All he'd need to do is watch, and when he sees the time is right, return. He's probably feeling desperate now Fanny is locked up and no longer doing his bidding."

I'd given it a lot of thought, and the more I did, the stronger the possibility that I was right grew.

Knox bent down, grabbed a rock, and threw it at the bird. "I think this is a case where it's better to kill the messenger."

When the stone missed its target, the raven let out a loud screech and retreated to a different tree away from the inn's property. It wouldn't remain gone forever, but for the next few moments, it couldn't watch for any news.

"How is she?" His question revealed how nervous he was. "Has anyone come down to let you know how things are?"

I started laughing. "I'm pretty confident if I knock on that door one more time, Madame Luiza will begin throwing rocks at me too."

That got a reaction out of him. "Being a nuisance, huh?" Knox chuckled, casting another look up to our room. "Maybe I should go up and ask? I haven't worn out my welcome yet. I should be safe."

I shrugged my shoulders. "I wouldn't risk it. Those two mean business up there. Nothing short of the inn burning to the ground will make those women relent. It's what's best for Catriona and the baby. That's the only reason why I didn't force myself in there to stay."

There was no way I'd jeopardize the birth.

Knox chewed on the inside of his cheek. He had something on his mind, but knowing I wouldn't leave my wife alone obviously posed a problem.

"What is it?" I asked, my curiosity finally piqued. "Tell me what's got you so excited, and once I know everything's okay, I'll go with you to see whatever it is. Deal?"

I was so sure that nothing he said could convince me otherwise, I almost dropped to the ground when he told me his good news—information that saw me abandoning my post and running after him.

Knox. My wonderful Phineas had somehow managed the impossible.

He'd found a cure for my curse.

Within the hour, if all went well, I would be able to welcome my child into the world.

As a man.

A *human* man.

My time as a blood drinker was finally going to come to an end.

CHAPTER 13

*J*could hear the rushing sound of the waterfall long before we stepped out from among the trees. An involuntary gasp escaped my lips. Even though I'd been told that this place held strong elemental magic, it did nothing to prepare me for the breathtaking sight before me.

The bold colors instantly dazzled me, and the scents that wafted throughout the air were as intoxicating as the blood I craved.

"Have you ever seen such perfection?" Knox whispered, and I couldn't tell whether he was also caught up in the scenery, or if his remark was directed to the woman who stood quietly at the water's edge.

With the sun still high in the sky, her figure all but glowed as it emanated a softness that revealed she wasn't human. Her golden hair fell down below her waist, and while there wasn't a breeze to be felt, strands that looked like fine-spun silk danced about around her.

The mystery woman wore a delicate cream dress that rivaled the beauty of her fair skin. Whoever she was, the crown of blue and white flowers that were laced together on top of her head paled in comparison, and I hadn't even seen her face yet. With her back to us, all I could imagine was this was truly an enchantress.

More importantly, this was the bestower of a great gift—the one to give me back my life.

"Who is she, Knox?" I asked, unable to tear my gaze around her.

"She's Unseelie," he murmured, awe filling each breath he exhaled. "She appeared while I was here picking burdock root. One minute I was alone, and the next I could hear the tinkling of her voice."

Fae.

There was no telling the true intention of this woman, but one glance at Knox, and I could see he was besotted by her. He believed she was the answer to our prayers, so for him, I would humor the meeting.

"You've returned to me, Phineas." A warm, delicious wave skirted over my skin as her voice was carried over the breeze. "Are you ready to strike our agreement?"

When she finally turned about, it was evident why she held such power over my friend. If I hadn't prepared myself—if Catriona didn't already own my heart—I would've walked through fire for this creature. Beautiful wasn't even the right word to describe her. Ethereal, exquisite—there was nothing in the human language that came close.

He nodded, and stepping to the side, introduced me to her. "Yralli, may I present my kin, Marcus St. James. It's for him that I ask a favor of you. It is his curse that I humbly beg you remove."

Her gaze turned to me, and the effect felt like a piercing blow to my soul. Whatever magic she was performing, the moment her eyes narrowed to study me, I felt everything strip away—who I was, my fears and insecurities, my hopes and dreams. Nothing was left untouched by her scrutiny, and while I knew it would be disastrous to offend her, it was hard not to resent the invasion.

"Your friend thinks very highly of you, Marcus St. James. It is not often I meet with a human who ignores his own wants and desires and places another before himself. He tells me you suffer from a gypsy curse, that you are damned to be a blood drinker for the rest of your days." Her slender fingers trailed along the tops of the tall grass that grew by the water. The long-stemmed flowers that appeared to grow almost instantly beside her bowed their heads in reverence. Nature seemed to worship the fae. If she actually healed me, I would bend at the knee as well.

"I've been fortunate enough to know such a man as Knox," I answered honestly. "There've been times I wondered whether I deserved such loyalty. Especially now, in your presence."

My response pleased her. "Do you understand what has passed between him and me?"

The sun's rays encompassed her as she came closer. Even though I could see the tips of her feet beneath her long flowing dress, it wouldn't have surprised me if she was floating on air. Each movement she made was filled with an otherworldly grace and elegance. It was impossible not to feel overwhelmed watching her— to feel unbelievably unclean.

"I will explain it to him afterwards," Knox interjected, and for the first time since approaching the waterfall, he looked at me. I couldn't quite recognize the emotion that filled his gaze, but before I could question him, he continued speaking. "Before him now, as my witness, I agree to your terms, Yralli, freely and without coercion."

"What terms?" I pressed, suddenly worried that whatever price she required to perform the healing would be too high, and one I would never ask him to give. "Knox. Please, what have you done?"

"Do you trust me?" was his response.

I didn't need to think. Nodding, I searched his features for some kind of hint. "With my life. You know that. You are the one I trust most above all else." I turned to face him completely. "Now please explain."

I didn't care what he'd promised this creature. This was my life that would change, and it was up to me to strike the deal if I didn't like his answer.

"She's agreed to make you human again."

Yralli spoke up now. She was within arm's reach now, and the magic emanating from her caused the air to ripple around us. It almost felt too stifling and oppressive to breathe.

"I will do this for you, for Phineas, on the condition that for the rest of your natural life, you spill no more blood. You will become human again and forgo your thirst for vengeance. Your enemies will continue to walk the earth. They will not be killed by your hand."

The agreement seemed simple enough, but I couldn't quite shake the stories that I'd heard—of hidden agendas and fae trickery. If something appeared too good to be true, it often was.

"And you believe this?" I asked, questioning Knox. "You accept her words at face value?"

An earnestness filled his features as he placed his hand on my shoulder. "With my whole heart. I know what you're thinking, Marcus, that she can't be trusted, but I wouldn't make this decision lightly. The seer told us we would find what we were seeking in Havenwood Falls, and it didn't just mean Catriona. One of the few portals that connect this world with Faerie is beyond these waterfalls. It's part of what gives this town, this land such power."

I gripped his hand and squeezed it. I knew he was being sincere, but I couldn't let him risk himself on my behalf. "But her intentions?"

There was a touch of coldness in Yralli's tone. "Do you question my honor, blood drinker?" Her using that title with me was a stark reminder that the future of my curse was hanging in the balance and relied heavily on the outcome of this conversation. "Tell me, how have you fared in finding those who cursed you? Do you know the true nature of these beings and how they are able to hide in the shadows, evading you?"

Her words confused me. "True nature? They are mere humans —gypsies who practice limited magic."

Her laughter teased my ears. "There is nothing simple and limited about the power they yield. I can see their magic woven in the very fibers of your being. I see the truth of their enchantment. You will not be freed from your curse so easily, Marcus St. James. Mark my warning. Finding them will only bring your ruination and despair. Are you willing to lose all you hold dear because your pride dictates it?"

She had seen through my hesitation. This fae had peered into my mind and seen my fear of her.

"And all you ask of me is that I not shed any more blood?" I repeated part of the deal to her, hoping that if there was some kind of deceit, the truth would be revealed.

"Yes. This is how you will make amends for the deaths you are responsible for. A balance must be returned to nature. Her cries and tears demand it."

It couldn't be that simple, but I found myself beginning to believe her.

"And you think this is our only option, Knox?" I asked. He was the one who took on the responsibility of finding a cure through his alchemy. He had sworn to never leave my side until he'd restored my humanity, and it was hard to ignore the hope I felt radiating off him. The feeling went beyond him being enraptured by her beauty.

"I have searched the world, studying until my head has throbbed. I have experimented with elements until exhausting every shred of knowledge I've obtained, but only found failure. Catriona is right now giving birth to a child—a baby that will become yours. Can you not see how plausible this solution is and how perfectly this encounter is timed?"

His conviction pierced my skepticism, and my mind wandered back to the inn, where my wife was ready to deliver either a son or a daughter. What kind of father would I be if there was always a threat of losing control of my bloodlust? What if something happened and I did the unforgivable?

That truth, more than anything, left me with the only choice I could accept.

"Then I graciously accept your gift, Yralli," I said, her name rolling off my tongue like a melody. "And I swear on my restored life that I will never spill the blood of others again."

As the words left my body, I could almost see the magic touch them, making my oath visible to the eye in a glittery silver script. I had just made a deal with a dark fae.

I could only hope that I hadn't just invited more trouble into my life.

CHAPTER 14

"It is done."

One moment I was standing, bracing myself to feel the magic rushing through my veins, and the next I dropped to my knees, screaming. The pain that I'd experienced when the curse was first cast was nothing compared to the agony that torched my insides, incinerating everything it touched. Over and over, I clawed the ground around me, desperate to escape the pain.

My vision clouded to where there was nothing but darkness. Blinded and sobbing, I curled myself up into the fetal position and prayed that I would survive this. All I could do was picture Catriona in my mind—her beautiful smile, the way her eyes lit up whenever something pleased her. I was doing this for her—for our new child—and most of all, for me.

This was my chance to right the wrong done to me. It was a fresh start for someone who yearned for normalcy. I didn't care what I was giving up. I'd had my fill of fury and revenge. All it had done was bring bitterness and isolation to my life. The curse had cast me into shadow and blood. I was ready to say goodbye to damnation forever.

I couldn't stop screaming as fae magic ravaged my soul. Somewhere in the back of my mind, I knew Knox was watching. Did he view this as the freedom that I did? Was he also ready to be released from the oath he'd sworn to me?

Each thought crashed and burned around me. Nothing else mattered. All there was—all I could feel—was this moment. This blistering moment.

My body began convulsing, slamming hard to the ground as wave after wave left me shaking. Gasping for breath, I dug my nails into the dirt, anything that would help me find some way to control the process. Everything hurt. My muscles twisted and contorted like they had a mind of their own.

Then with one last, drawn out scream, I finally saw the light at the end of the tunnel. The pain began to ebb and gradually diminish. Sweat dripped from my body. Fast trickles of salty water ran across my face, clinging to the tip of my nose before spilling onto the ground.

With ragged breath, weakened, I grunted. The spell was completed, and I was beyond exhausted. If it wasn't for the fact that Catriona was waiting for me to return, I would have feebly found the strength to cover myself with dirt, burying myself. Death had felt so close.

"Marcus," came Knox's voice through the muddied fog that surrounded me. "My God, talk to me." He gently laid one of his hands over my arm, and I buckled beneath his touch. Everything felt tender and sore.

I'd grown so accustomed to being a vampire—to the benefits that came from existing on blood and the power it gave me. Each second that passed proved one thing.

I was human again.

I was mortal, and the fading pain was proof.

"I'm fine," I eventually stammered. My body felt strange, and panic fluttered when I couldn't quite move my limbs properly. It was as if there was still a disconnect between my body and brain. "I think."

My lashes flickered open, the light causing a throb to explode behind my eyes. Once they adjusted, I stared straight up into my friend's worried face. His blond hair hung straight down like a curtain. "I thought she was going to kill you! Was that what it was like when you were cursed?"

Licking my dry lips, trying to swallow to alleviate my sore throat, I shook my head. "This . . . this was much worse." And it was. The only difference was that I'd blacked out before. This time I'd been disturbingly aware of everything. "But it worked."

And that made it worth it.

Cradling my head in his lap, Knox was hesitant to move me. "No more bloodlust?"

I reached out within myself for the sensations I'd lived with for way too many years. Nothing. No beast. No ravaging need to gorge myself on blood.

"I'm human." A burst of laughter erupted from me. Despite the agony, there was a new emotion that surfaced.

Joy.

I was finally free. I could let go of the monster and find myself again.

Gradually, Knox helped me to my feet, and I slowly began moving my body. It really was intoxicating to not have that urge and need to feed constantly pulling my focus.

"Thank you," I exclaimed, and I threw my arms around him in an embrace. "You said you wouldn't rest until you found a way, and you did it. Thank you, brother."

He pounded my back with his hand affectionately. "No, we did it."

A soft twittering sound came from behind me, a reminder that we weren't alone in our celebration. Staggering around, I grinned so hard I was surprised it didn't crack my face.

"I am in your debt, Yralli," I declared, grateful for her magic. I still didn't quite understand why she would grant such a wish where the only requirement was a promise. She gained nothing directly from helping me. Yet, there she stood in benevolence, her hands gracefully grasped before her.

"As long as you honor your word, Marcus St. James, no debt is required from you. I have received what I yearn for." And her gaze drifted over to Knox.

Something passed between them—unspoken words—and seeing the way Knox's face paled triggered a spark of anxiety.

What had he done? What was I missing?

"Marcus," he began, his own smile dwindling beneath his now unsure expression. "There's something I must tell you."

I glanced back and forth, not liking where this might lead. A shimmering portal appeared beside the water, and with it came a sinking sensation.

"No," I muttered, reaching for him. "Whatever it is, I don't want to hear it. We need to return to town and see whether Catriona has given birth. She'll be eager to see us." When he wouldn't budge and instead, bit his bottom lip, I threw my focus toward the fae.

"Whatever he's done, the agreement was between you and me. The bargain was to free me from the curse. Nothing else was mentioned."

Yralli simply stood there, the sun encasing her in a glowing light.

"No!" I repeated to Knox. "No."

"I owed you a life debt, Marcus. I saw an opportunity and took it. Whatever the sacrifice. Remember?" I could see he was trying to make me understand, but I refused to acknowledge the nagging feeling that wouldn't leave me be.

"Think of Catriona," I said, leading him away from the water and portal. With each step, my heart pounded inside my chest. All I could feel was an impending sense of doom. "She needs you, brother. The baby will need you." The words choked in my throat. "I need you."

The sadness in his smile broke my heart. "You're a family now. What more could you possibly want for?" Gripping my hand, Knox loosened my hold and took a step back toward Yralli. "I am only as strong as my word. You once said that, and I've used it as a marker for how I conduct myself."

"No," I countered. "All I have been is a monster. Stay. Let me show the man you and Catriona have inspired me to be. Brother. Do not leave."

That was what the thoughts screaming in my head were telling me—the truth that I was desperate to deny and prove false. The deal I'd made with the fae was but a pittance in comparison to the secret oath Knox had made.

A life for a life.

I begged him to tell me I was wrong. "Please." Never had I sounded so needy and devastated. "Knox."

All he could do was shake his head. Sorrow filled his eyes. All while the fae witnessed the rift she'd caused between us.

Just as I was ready to unleash my anger toward her, a crack of branches from nearby footsteps drew my attention. Knox turned about to see what was causing the interruption.

"You!" he thundered, the change in his voice as different as night and day. Gone was the heartfelt need for me to accept this was his decision. In its place, a look of wrath descended, and he curled his hands into fists.

"I thank you for conveniently being together and away from

prying eyes." A dark-haired man stood smirking at us, and it only took a few moments to realize who he was.

Dark hair.

European descendant.

A knowing look when his gaze fell on me.

This was the bastard who had stolen Catriona from under our noses that night of the attack. It had been dark when he'd ridden off with her, but I would've recognized that face anywhere.

He'd come back for her.

He'd returned to face our retribution.

"You're a fool if you think you're leaving this place alive," I growled, my perfectly honed anger rising inside me. "Prepare to meet your maker."

He strode closer with all the swagger of someone who felt no fear. "I could say the same for you both. Imagine my surprise when I arrived in Havenwood Falls and found you both had left my Catriona unprotected." The way he emphasized *my* made my skin crawl. "My pet brought news that she's about to give birth. Such a pity you will never see them again."

The raven. I suspected there'd been something about that bird, and now we knew. All this time it had been watching us.

I didn't answer. I was done with talking about it, and the merry little dance Dimitri was doing in bragging about his intentions. I'd dreamt of this day, when I'd come face to face with the gypsy who'd taken my wife. He had a lot to atone for, and there was no way I'd allow him to continue breathing now we were together.

Rushing forward, I cocked back my fist and slammed it into his head. He'd seen me coming and had tried to meet me halfway. I didn't care that his own blows connected. All I could think—feel— was that I could finally get retribution on behalf of Catriona.

We fell to the ground and rolled about, each one trying to get the upper hand. At one stage I had him pinned, my hands wrapped firmly around his neck, but with one painful strike, Dimitri broke my stronghold. He twisted his body out from under me and stood to his feet.

"It will take much more than a slight tussle to kill me, Marcus." He spat to the side and wiped his mouth with the back of his hand. He quickly looked to where Knox was and gestured for him to approach. "I thought you vowed to be the one to end my life, Englishman."

Both Knox and I began stalking around the gypsy like he was our prey and we were superior predators. We didn't rush in or do anything hasty. We were united in one purpose. If we were ever to have a moment's peace and keep Catriona and the baby safe, we would need to end this fight here.

"Cowards!" he screeched, as an angry red vein throbbed at his temple. Dirt smudged his jaw, and his coat sleeve revealed a tear. "Perhaps you need to hear how I defiled your wife, Marcus. How I had her beneath me, screaming for help . . . screaming for you to rescue her."

I couldn't stand to hear another word. With murderous intent, I lunged at Dimitri, clawing at him with a savagery even my time as a vampire hadn't produced. All I could think was this man—this animal—needed to be destroyed.

In the back of my mind, I could hear Knox yelling for me to stop. Hands grabbed me and attempted to pull me off the gypsy, but I couldn't be reasoned with. Dimitri had found my weakness, the one thing that could've unraveled my self-control and rendered me a beast again.

Catriona.

Image after image of her tear-stained face, beseeching me to stop her assailant from raping her, appeared before my eyes. I could hear my name reverberating in my ears—the anguish and utter desolation that filled her voice. I had failed her so completely.

How would she ever forgive me, let alone let me back into her heart?

"Monster!" I slammed my fist into his face. "She was innocent. Innocent," I repeated. With each word I cursed him like the braggart he was. There would be no redemption for him. No mercy shown, either.

"Your oath!" Knox said, finally gaining enough leverage to pull me away. "Or have you forgotten so quickly?"

Shocked to find that I had, I turned quickly to where Yralli was still standing. She'd done nothing to lift her hand and help. Instead, she watched on in veiled boredom.

I couldn't give full rein to my anger.

I wouldn't be able to have the satisfaction of ripping this brute into pieces.

No blood could be spilled. Not by my hand. Not from me.

By accepting my humanity and enjoying the first moments in what felt like a lifetime as a man, I had also ensured that Dimitri couldn't die from my efforts.

With a heaving chest, my breath ragged from overexertion, I cursed with disappointment.

"Grant me another favor," I demanded from the silent fae. "You must be aware of what this man is to me and how he has harmed my family. Grant me an exception, and I will give you whatever you want." I couldn't stop pacing from the adrenaline that pulsed thickly through my veins.

When she didn't respond, I looked to Knox. "You have a rapport with this creature. Strike another bargain. Do whatever is necessary so that this fiend's threat is extinguished."

Dimitri started laughing. The sound was filled with derision. He was seeing a chance to escape the death sentence he deserved. "Only a fool would strike an accord with the fae. Intervening is beneath such cold and callous beings. Face me and accept that once the life has drained from your eyes, I will take your wife and my child. I will bury you alongside your naïve friend."

He slipped out of his coat, and quickly rolling up his sleeves, the gypsy began toward us again.

I weighed my options.

If I drew blood and killed him, I would also return to being a blood drinker. The existence I'd had to endure would come crashing back, and in all honesty, take away any chance of being cured. I knew the odds of finding the clan responsible. I'd spent so much time hunting them that I'd ignored the fact that they also held the power to remain hidden.

Was my humanity truly worth my thirst for revenge?

Knox didn't wait for me to act. He had made his own decision and, with his fingers curled around a gold bladed knife, slashed at Dimitri—the razor-sharp edge slicing across his throat. Blood began to gush from the wound, and no amount of pressure from the gypsy's hand could stem the reality that it was a fatal blow.

Blood gurgled up through his throat and out of his mouth. With wide, dark eyes, Dimitri staggered forward only to fall heavily to his knees.

I stared at Knox, noting the spray of blood that had struck his face. In that moment, I remembered the young boy he'd been when I found him in London and witnessed the man he'd become. A muscle in his jaw twitched from his clenched teeth, and as Dimitri took his last breath and slumped to the side, Knox released his death grip on the knife.

"It is done," he uttered, not realizing he'd just said the same thing as Yralli had. "It is over."

I looked down at the knife. Intricate scrollwork was etched alongside the top of the blade, and the hilt was made from deer antler. I'd never seen the weapon before, but when it twinkled out of existence, I knew exactly where it had come from.

A slight nod from Yralli confirmed my suspicion. She'd stepped in to help Knox and end the attack. While she hadn't granted me the right to avenge my wife, the fae had given aid nevertheless.

"Phineas," she spoke, "you must say your goodbyes."

I shook my head. Not now. Not just yet. There was so much to say and do before that. All I needed was a chance to find a way to break his promise. I refused to allow this to be our last moment together.

My mind was made up. "Remove my humanity," I ordered. "Take it from me and give me back the blood lust. The price is too high. He is mine. You cannot have him."

Moving to stand in front of Knox, I held my arms out to the side, blocking him from her.

Her gaze narrowed so dramatically that I felt an icy cold breeze blast me. She waved her hand through the air, and as pain gripped me once more, her thundering voice filled the air. "Vow breaker."

A tremor coursed through me, and then to my horror, a familiar sensation flowed into me, filling the deepest recesses of my soul.

"Nooooo!" I cried in agony, clutching my sides as I desperately tried to escape the onslaught. Hunger like nothing I'd ever experienced flared, and all I could focus on was my thirst for blood. I wanted to bathe in it, drown in the simplicity and power. My body contorted so under the demand to feed that I worried my limbs would shatter beneath the unrelenting pressure.

"Yralli!" Knox cried, rushing toward her. "He's broken no vow! Why have you done this?" He reached for her, only for the fae to disappear a second before he could touch her. She reappeared beside Dimitri and pointed down to his lifeless body.

"Blood has been shed. Our agreement has been nullified."

With what little strength I had, I crawled my way to the body, desperate to see if what she was saying was true. I hadn't been the one to wield the knife. I had punched him, strangled him, but as far as I had seen—no blood had been spilt. At least not by my hand.

I tugged on the gypsy, moving his body and limbs about to study him closer. Everywhere I looked, I found bruises and red welts, but no blood.

It wasn't until Knox joined me and flipped the body onto his back, that the truth proved undeniable. There was the faintest of scratches along the dead man's hairline. It had yielded the tiniest speck of blood. If I hadn't peered so close, I would've easily assumed it was dirt.

Yralli was right.

I had without intention broken my vow.

My humanity was stripped away.

I was a blood drinker once more.

CHAPTER 15

I hadn't known what hope felt like until I stood there, having watched it evaporate before me. In the blink of an eye, my world had brightened, only to be reduced to shadows again.

It wasn't fair.

The bitterness that coated my tongue and filled my mouth was hard to swallow. All I could do was pray that this had all been some brutal nightmare—a twisted dream.

"Knox," I uttered. "Tell me this isn't happening."

He looked equally distraught. "In order to strike the deal, I had to offer her what she wanted. Even though her agreement with you is broken, ours still holds."

I looked over to the fae, who wisely remained silent. The portal had reappeared, shimmering and glittering behind her.

"How long?" I asked, staring at the opening that would lead to another world—one where I couldn't follow. "Please tell me you didn't blindly accept her terms. You provided yourself a way out?"

Here was a man who I knew could negotiate himself out of even the strangest of situations. There was a reason why I trusted him with not only my estate's affairs, but also my own. I couldn't imagine him locking himself into an ironclad contract without some kind of loophole.

He gave me a look as if my doubting him was offensive. "Ten years. I promised her my companionship for a decade, and once that time is over, I'm free to return. She's agreed to arrange safe passage back to Havenwood Falls."

Ten years. I could handle that. This wasn't a forever goodbye. While I still felt like I'd been tricked to accept the bargain, it wasn't as though Knox was about to completely disappear into Faerie.

I nodded my head and let out a sigh of relief. "I'll miss you, brother."

He pulled me against him and clapped his hand over my back. "Try not to get into trouble while I'm gone." He squeezed me tightly. I did the same. I knew that once he let go, he would need to leave. "I won't stop looking. Even though I won't be here, perhaps there's an answer to your curse in Faerie."

Even now he was thinking of me instead of himself.

"Forget about my curse, Knox. I've lived with it for this long. Perhaps it's time to accept that this is who I am and embrace it." Tears stung my eyes. He blinked back his own.

His voice broke as he struggled to get out the words. "Brothers. Always. I still owe you a life debt. I will never stop searching."

Our embrace ended, our eyes locking in silent communication. Promises were exchanged. Encouragement and love were shown. We'd been through so much. This wouldn't be the end of a friendship that had been forged in strength and loyalty.

"I'll tell my child about you. Catriona and I will be waiting here for you."

"You'd better." He chuckled, already backing away. Right before he breached the portal, Knox turned to wave. "Until then."

And then he was gone. I'd blinked, hoping to call out one more time, but the shimmering flickered before fading away to nothing. I was left there alone—a dead body on the ground, and the splash of the waterfall filling the air.

I don't know how long I remained there, staring at the spot I'd last seen Knox. The threat to Catriona had also been taken care of, leaving me with only one thing to do.

I was about to become a father.

Blood drinker or not, I owed this child only the best version of myself.

And that's what I would do.

I had faced the blood and embraced damnation.

Wrath had all but consumed me as I focused solely on my need for retribution.

But as I walked slowly back to town and was greeted with the joyous news that Catriona had delivered a healthy baby girl, I knew that those things could never be allowed into my heart again.

Not now.

Not ever.

Hope and love. Those would be the virtues I clung to.

For Catriona.

For Knox.

For me.

I was Marcus St. James, and in the wake of loss and heartbreak, I would rise.

EPILOGUE

KNOX

*T*ime moved slowly here. Painstakingly slow.

Once Yralli had taken me through the portal, the beauty that had held me mesmerized quickly evolved into something less enchanting and intoxicating.

I was her captive for the next ten years, but what she'd failed to confess—what I had failed to ask—was that here in Faerie, time almost stood still, while the world I left behind marched forward at a steady pace.

I knew returning to the spot where my life changed was foolish and nothing but pure torture. Yralli mocked the sentiment, her once tinkling voice now filled with derision and scorn. She'd wanted me simply for the sake of claiming me, and where I thought I might've had some freedom, I was nothing more than a pet to her.

A possession.

A toy to pleasure and satisfy her every whim and desire.

A week had passed since I followed her and said goodbye to Marcus. The illusion she'd magically created to lure me had already begun to wear thin, but I refused to show her that I could see her for what she truly was.

It was why I always came back here. It drew me like a siren and reminded me why I'd made the deal and what I was fighting for. Marcus had deserved a shot at true happiness. He needed to know that he didn't have to be the monster he believed himself to be.

They came every week to the waterfall. With a basket of food and blanket in hand, the family I missed made the slow walk through the woods to the place that held so many memories.

It was there that I learned that Catriona had given birth to a beautiful daughter. The sound of her name still echoed in my ears from the moment Marcus had said it.

Esther.

It meant star.

There was no denying that this bundle of joy had shone a light into their lives, giving Marcus something to hold on to, a reason to let go of his darkness.

My arms longed to breach the barrier that kept us apart and gather Esther up. I wanted to witness her first smile and celebrate as she spoke her first words. I would miss all of that—milestones that cemented their little family together.

I wondered whether I would find myself at home in their presence once my time was over and I could return to their world. How changed would I be? Would they even be alive when the ten years were over?

"Should I be jealous?" came her voice from over my shoulder. "Do you regret the sacrifice of love you made?" Yralli had revealed her own weakness whenever she found me here, waiting for my family to show up. Human emotions intrigued her, and for some reason, she wanted to understand.

"I stand by my choice," I answered. In my mind, I'd exchanged one master for another. "There's nothing I wouldn't do for my brother." Those words rang as true as the day I'd made the bargain.

"Even if it means you must always watch from a distance?" She crept closer, as if hoping she could somehow see what I did. "Does this not make you lonely?"

I shook my head, not quite sure how I could explain my reasoning. "It helps me stay connected. Seeing them happy and together reminds me to never give up hope." A smile curled the ends of my lips as Esther played with her father's fingers. I would never grow tired of seeing my dear friend soften around his daughter—the way everything seemed to melt away whenever he looked at her. She was the miracle. She was why I knew I'd had to give whatever Yralli asked for.

Esther needed Marcus and vice versa.

"Come," the woman said. The command came with the same musical tone, but it also held the warning that her patience was growing thin. There was only so much she would tolerate before the fae would reveal her darker nature. That was a side of her I hoped never to see directed my way.

Her treatment of the other human she held captive was enough to give me nightmares every time I closed my eyes.

With one last longing glance, I offered up a silent prayer of protection over Marcus and his family.

Don't forget me, I whispered, as I reluctantly followed Yralli back to the palace.

I was bound to a princess of the Unseelie Court.

God give me the strength to survive it.

We hope you enjoyed this story in the Legends of Havenwood Falls series featuring a variety of supernatural creatures. The series is a collaborative effort by multiple authors.

Other Havenwood Falls books by Belinda:

Nowhere to Hide
Addicted to You
The Collector: Awakening
Blood and Damnation
Sun & Moon Academy Book One: Fall Semester
Sun & Moon Academy Book Two: Spring Semester

Books in the historical Legends of Havenwood Falls series:

Lost in Time by Tish Thawer
Dawn of the Witch Hunters by Morgan Wylie
Redemption's End by Eric R. Asher
Trapped Within a Wish by Brynn Myers
Blood and Damnation by Belinda Boring
Fated Beginnings by E.J. Fechenda
Emeline by Katie M. John
Released From a Curse by Brynn Myers
A Pack of Lies by Kallie Ross
Kiss the Ashes by Desiree Lafawn
Hidden Truths by Colleen Nye
Wrath and Retribution by Belinda Boring
Changing Fate by Char Webster
Rise of the Witch Hunters by Morgan Wylie
The Drowning Bride by Seven Jane

Also try the main Havenwood Falls series; the YA line, Havenwood Falls High; the darker, sexier side of town, Havenwood Falls Sin & Silk; and the local supernatural college, Sun & Moon Academy.

Stay up to date at www.HavenwoodFalls.com

Subscribe to our reader group and receive free stories and more!

ABOUT THE AUTHOR

International and #1 multi-genre bestselling Author Belinda Boring is known to many readers as the Queen of Swoon and also the Queen of Cliffhangers. Her Mystic Wolves series has topped many charts along with receiving several awards and nominations such as Paranormal Book of the Year, Best Debut Book, as well as being in the Top 3 Best Rated on Amazon. With additional titles like *Bittersweet Melody*, *Bittersweet Symphony*, *Enchanted Hearts*, *Loving Liberty* and *Broken Promises*, it's easy to see why readers are captivated by this swoon worthy author! You can also find Belinda writing alongside the incredible authors of the Havenwood Falls world. To date, she's published within their main Havenwood Falls line, as well as sharing the past tales of characters within the Legends of Havenwood Falls.

A homesick Aussie living amongst the cactus and mountains of Arizona, Belinda Boring is a self-proclaimed addict of romance and all things swoon worthy. It wasn't long before she began writing, pouring her imagination and creativity into the stories she dreams. Whether urban fantasy, paranormal romance, or romance in general, Belinda strives to share great plots with heart and characters that you can't help but connect with. Of course, she wouldn't be Belinda without adding heroes she hopes will curl your toes. Surrounded by a supportive cast of family, friends, two adorable Chiweenies, and the man she gives her heart and soul to, Belinda is living the good life. Happy reading!

ACKNOWLEDGMENTS

"Gratitude unlocks the fullness of life. It turns what we have into enough, and more. It turns denial into acceptance, chaos to order, confusion to clarity. It can turn a meal into a feast, a house into a home, a stranger into a friend."

– Melody Beattie

Whenever I finish a story, I'm reminded just how fortunate I am for the supportive people in my life. I'm grateful that I can pursue my dreams and give voice to my imagination because I know I don't have to do it alone. From a loving husband, to close family and friends, to the group of incredible authors and gracious readers . . . I'm lifted up and inspired by their acts of kindness and encouraging words. While writing can often be a solitary task, if you look closely, you can see their tendrils of faith and loyalty that add fuel to the author's dream. I love my tribe. I love each of the hearts and minds that stand with me throughout each book. I'd be lost without them. I am better because of them. Thank you from the bottom of my heart. I hope I continue to make you all proud.

"It's not where you are in life, it's who you have by your side that matters."

– Unknown

Bels xoxo

AN EXCERPT

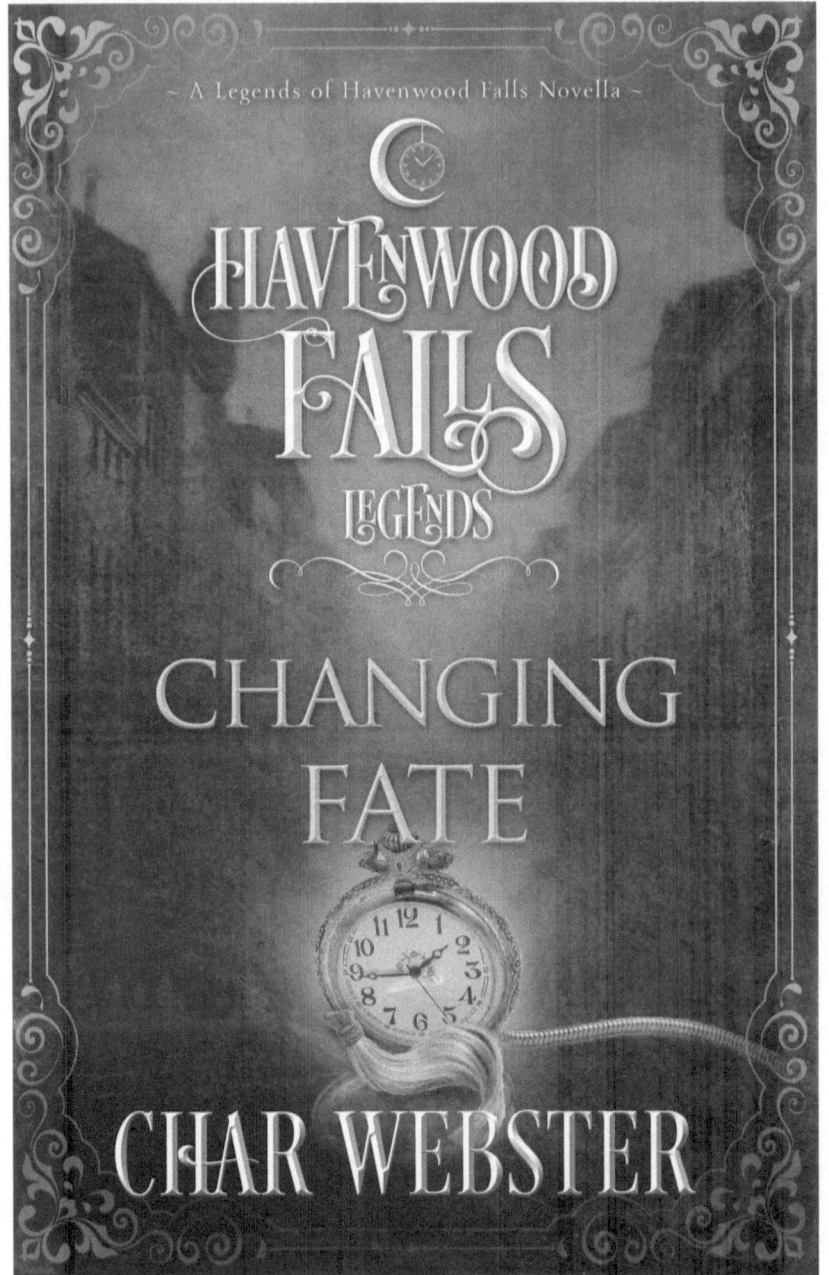

~ A Legends of Havenwood Falls Novella ~

HAVENWOOD FALLS LEGENDS

CHANGING FATE

CHAR WEBSTER

Changing Fate (A Legends of Havenwood Falls Novella) by Char Webster

From this *USA Today* Bestselling Author - For a vila warrior, love only comes with death.

During World War I, vila warrior Jerina Ventus's life irrevocably changed when she saved a wounded soldier's life and helped him return to his hometown in Colorado. Twenty-five years later, she's restless and longing for another adventure beyond her forest. Little does she know, her sister Kosa will deliver the opportunity to her.

Thane Beltaine grew up hearing stories about the beautiful and fierce immortal warrior who saved his father's life. When Jerina's sister Kosa shows up in his hometown on the arm of a wicked mage, Thane volunteers to find Jerina and bring her back. He never expected to meet the woman who was more legend than real and definitely didn't think they would clash about every little thing.

Jerina's temper and patience are tested as they travel to Colorado to rescue her sister, who at first seems reluctant to be saved. She needs to outsmart the mage and find a way to release Kosa from his control, and she needs Thane's help to do this.

Reluctantly, they work together to save Kosa, and an unexpected love begins to grow. But vila are cursed to never find true love—if they do, he will quickly die a gruesome death.

CHANGING FATE

BY CHAR WEBSTER

Obnoxious laughter followed Jerina's ungraceful and rapid descent to the ground from the thick branch she had been perched upon. With a wave of her hands, gusts of wind pushed up against her free fall, slowing her plummet to a slight drop and landing her lightly on her feet.

Her sister, Kosa, was still cackling like a hyena when Jerina stalked over to her. Scooping up a handful of snow, she dumped it on Kosa's blond head in retribution for the snow blast her sister sent to knock her out of the tree. The icy shower coated her soft leather handmade jacket.

Kosa shook the snow from her long straight hair. "I've never caught you unaware! You should have seen your face when you fell."

Jerina growled at Kosa. "You should be patrolling, not messing around!"

The sisters faced each other with the same graceful height, same lithe build, and same long blond hair. Even though there were a few years separating them, they could nearly pass for twins.

"My shift is finished. You would know that if you hadn't been pouting in that tree!" Kosa prepared herself for Jerina to attack. This was a fight that had been brewing for years.

Jerina swung out with her fist, but Kosa ducked out of the way while thrusting her leg out to trip her sister.

The girls ended up in a tangle of long arms and legs as they rolled across the forest floor, kicking up snow and leaves in their fury. They ignored the fierce growl that continued to gain in volume but were pulled apart when sharp teeth sank into the soft leather of Jerina's left boot.

"Damn it, Rela! If you tear my boots, I'm going to send you off to the next country!" Jerina yelled at the regal mountain lion that was still growling and showing lethal fangs. Rela was not intimidated in the least by her outburst. The mountain lion shook her head while still grasping Jerina's brown suede boot, making sure the girls knew she wasn't going to let go until they stopped fighting.

Jerina raised her hands, and wind started to whip through the trees, blowing the mountain lion's fur, but she stood firm. Sighing dramatically, Jerina released Kosa and fell back onto the forest floor, breathing heavily.

Rela dropped the boot with what sounded like a snort, but she stood close to the sisters, making sure they didn't continue to brawl.

Kosa ruffled the velvety tan fur of their good friend. "You could have waited a little longer before interrupting us."

Jerina glared at her sister. "Why are you picking a fight today, Kos?"

"You have not been yourself for years, not since you returned from your trip, but lately it's become far more severe. What is the matter?" Kosa wasn't the only one to notice the change in Jerina. Their mother had begun to ask questions, and that was never good.

Rela's head was leaning over Jerina's shoulder as she sat up, so she pushed it out of the way. It sounded like Rela was laughing at her. She was about to reply that nothing was wrong but decided to speak the truth. "I find myself restless."

"You've always been content here in our forest." Kosa was the one who would seek adventure whenever possible.

Rela settled down on some soft moss, not minding the patches of snow, and closed her eyes, ignoring them since they had stopped fighting.

"I love it, but . . ."

"You need something more," Kosa finished for her.

"Yes!" Jerina whipped her hands up, creating a cyclone of leaves, sticks, snow, and wind around the three of them. "I feel as if I should be doing something, but I do not know what."

"We could venture into town and find some humans to have fun with." Kosa had been sneaking off to town whenever she could, but she didn't want her sister to know how often.

Jerina narrowed her gaze. "What have you done?"

"We are not speaking about me. We are discussing your melancholy mood." Kosa was not going to let Jerina intimidate her.

"You know we cannot become attached to humans."

Kosa rolled her eyes. "We cannot get involved with anyone." Kosa spread her hands out wide, and the cyclone stopped. Everything rained down to the ground in a flurry of debris. "No one is around to hear us. You don't need to draw unwanted attention to this area."

"Kosa, I've seen the little gifts that are left for you."

Kosa's eyes grew round, but she smoothed her shock away and tried to act casual. "I have happened upon a few trinkets. They don't mean anything. They could have been left for anyone."

Jerina raised an eyebrow. "Who is he?"

Kosa had no idea how the conversation shifted to Jerina interrogating her. "I don't have any idea what you're talking about."

"Kos."

"Maybe you should go back and visit Tannor."

"Your attempt at diverting the conversation will not work. Tell me about him." Jerina didn't like the dreamy look in her sister's eyes. She also didn't want to talk about Tannor and her trip across the world. She felt drawn to Colorado but not romantically. She had developed a friendship with Tannor, and that was it. No deeper feelings were involved. Tannor loved his wife more than anything, and Jerina had helped him get back to her when he had been seriously injured.

"There is nothing to say." Kosa began to bounce in place, something she did when she was nervous and not being entirely truthful. She forced herself to stop and face Jerina. "I'd rather talk about you and why you have become insufferable lately."

Jerina thrust her hands toward her sister, and hurricane force winds blasted Kosa back several feet before Kosa diverted the gust upward. Jerina's glare would have scared some of the warrior trainees.

"Do not trifle with me." She stopped the wind when Rela roared.

Kosa cracked her neck back and forth. "You have been horrid to everyone, and you have been drifting off alone whenever you're not on duty."

Jerina sank down onto a fallen tree trunk. Her first reaction was to argue, but her sister's tone stopped her. "You should not exaggerate."

"Mother has noticed." Kosa had told their mother that some of the newer trainees had been goofing off instead of working hard, and that was the reason for Jerina's moodiness. It had only been half of the truth, but it had satisfied her.

Jerina pulled a stick from the log and picked at its bark. "I've been feeling a pull toward Colorado. I do not know why it's so strong after all these years."

Kosa sat down next to Jerina.

"I've been longing to travel." She knew it was the wrong thing to say as soon as it came out of her mouth.

"Tell me about the gifts and the man." Jerina narrowed her eyes at Kosa.

Kosa growled silently, cursing her big mouth. "You cannot let anyone know about this."

"Tell me at once." Jerina knew that a man had been leaving little things for her sister, but those gifts had become more frequent and more elaborate.

Kosa took a deep breath. It was time to explain everything to Jerina. Out of all the vila warriors, her sister was the only one who went out into the world and returned. Others had left, but only to find tragedy and heartache. Men were the downfall of the vila.

"I've been watching the humans in town. They fascinate me."

Jerina inhaled quickly. "Were you seen?"

"Not at first, but then I found a note pinned to the tree I take shelter behind."

"What did it say?" Jerina stood and began to pace the small clearing, scanning the area for anyone who might be listening to their conversation.

Kosa sighed wistfully. "It said, 'I thought only angels had the power to stop a man's heart.'"

Jerina rolled her eyes. "He was trying to charm you with pretty words."

"It was sweet." Kosa sighed again. "The next day, a white camellia was tied to the tree with another note. This one said, 'My destiny is in your hands.'"

"That sounds ominous." Jerina was starting to get worried. Something didn't feel right.

Purchase **Changing Fate** where books are sold.